The Listeners

Edward Parnell

RƎTHINK PRESS

PRAISE FOR 'THE LISTENERS'

'The use of multiple voices and viewpoints in *The Listeners* is deftly handled; all of the characters have their own individual pitch, and the way their stories interweave is precisely executed. In William Abrehart we have an almost forensic observer of the environment; William is the lynchpin of the narrative – a listener and an acute observer – but an unreliable witness, too, whose own heart-rending secret knowledge is gradually revealed to shocking effect. Edward Parnell has created an intense and powerful story filled with memorable characters. *The Listeners* is a very fine debut.'
　　—Trezza Azzopardi, author of *The Hiding Place* and
　　Winterton Blue

'Edward Parnell sets his story of family tragedy and domestic conflict among the quiet poetry of the everyday. It's the war and the Abreharts are trying to make peace with each other and with their past. *The Listeners* may be a first novel, but it is beautifully crafted and written with immense assurance. The story of Norfolk and of the Norfolk landscape has just found an exciting new voice.'
　　—Mark Cocker, author of *Crow Country* and
　　Birds Britannica, naturalist and columnist

'Set in Norfolk during the Second World War and woven around Walter de la Mare's famous poem of the same name, *The Listeners* moves through various narrators caught in their own dense, claustrophobic webs. This is a novel particularly rich and subtle in its sense of nature and in its haunting perception of the birds and woods in which a boy's imagination is invested. But who are the ghosts and who are the living? That is the trail of suspense that leads to the centre of the web.'
　　—George Szirtes, poet and translator, winner of the
　　T. S. Eliot Prize for Poetry

For my brother

And he felt in his heart their strangeness,
Their stillness answering his cry

Walter de la Mare, 'The Listeners'

May 25th 1940

WILLIAM

Up the stairs is a ghost house. Sun slants through the glassless windows, bathing the greying walls and pale spaces where pictures used to hang. No one comes here any more besides me, though when I was little we snuck inside to play and Rachel said if you concentrate hard you can catch them whispering from way back. We are the listeners, she told us, like in the poem. But we never did hear a sound, except for the beckoning branches, and once a stag coughing, which had me for a minute till I realised what it was.

Only later, on my own, did I make out the voice.

This, though, is different: something I have not seen here before. Silent, saying nothing, knowing everything, those empty eyes swallow me in; I do not think I will ever be able to look away, but my foot shuffles against the floorboards and, startled, it moth-flutters through the window's hollow gape.

I sink among the muck and dust; at least in here I am apart from Mother's stillness and Kate talking to me like I will forever be the smallest. Outside, the light lingers about the trees, soaking into the leaves as if they are marking where it happened. If I try my hardest to remember every single detail, the thoughts that craze my head may, finally, come right. Then I can try to make things better, help my mother and sisters become less sad. Because, even though he can no longer say, I think that is how he would want it.

Soon the house will go back to the wood and no one will realise it was ever anything but. First will come a blanket of bindweed, creeping through cracks in the floor. Ivy will grab the walls with never-let-go hooks, draping itself so thick that the stones beneath become a memory. Finally, the last slats of roof will surrender, releasing slender saplings to shoot skywards. The door has already fallen from its frame, half-hanging now, like the rotten bough that clings to the lightning-struck wych elm at the top of the drove. The deathwatches are stripping everything; it is becoming less and less of the place where he began and ended. I have not seen them, but their holes are drilled all about so I am certain they remain, hidden out of sight. Perhaps he caught a hint of their tapping right before I came upon him.

He is across at the church now. A year today since they covered him over, signing the spot with a cross of two sticks.

One whole year.

No name is written, but I watched them letting down the ropes so I know it is him.

Their hands move cautiously because they do not want to drop the box, all the while the Reverend going on in his special slow way he thinks God listens to.

'We commit his body to the ground.'

I am crying out and cannot catch the rest – something about being gloriously transformed – so try to run to where the dirt rains into the hole, only Big Jack holds me back. I shout, to make them realise that the Reverend is a liar, but my words come out jumbled and nobody gets what I want them to hear.

HOW CAN IT BE GLORIOUS? I try to say. How can it be when he is stuck down there, being broken apart by the worms and centipedes? How can anything be good now he is under the earth?

It is a BLOODY LIE.

My eyes open to the darkening sky. Someone is calling me.

William. William.

Could it be? I wonder if he will duck inside the doorway, so we can go home together and everything can be like before. Expectant, I wait, until I realise: I have been dreaming again.

He will not emerge from the trees.

I start back through the swaying shadows, coming into the meadow at the dip where the rainwater gathers, then skirt along the fence. It is quiet now, other than the birds singing their time-to-sleep songs – softly, so as not to stir themselves from their nearly-slumber. A movement ahead and a grey, hunched shape – a big lady sparrow hawk – scrabbles up off the grass. She glides away from me on angled-back wings, abandoning the still-warm carcass of a wood pigeon whose head she has picked clean. I think about taking what remains for the pot, as the rest is yet to be touched, but decide against. When I am out of her sight she can return and finish the job. If not, something else will come along in the night to clean up; already the feathers that soften the stiff outline are drifting across the damp pasture.

The cattle are filing back to the farm. Each evening at this time they begin their never-changing route. So regular how they tramp the same paths, like they cannot stray one step from where their hooves have always fallen. I will follow that way, presently, to where he is waiting.

Waiting for me to put things right.

RACHEL

My sister stretches ahead, desperate as always to outpace me. I feel disorientated, like a stranger – the parkland peculiar and out of place, the grass beneath the hornbeams a churned-up straggle of oats set down for the war effort. Why does nothing good remain the way it was? Will Tom even recognise any of this when he gets back?

I rise from the saddle and pedal harder, pulling alongside Kate as we pass through the open gates at the end of the drive; even at this distance the Hall squats over everything, ugly and square. We press on in silence, riding two abreast along the empty lanes in the waning sunlight. Approaching the house, I see Mother's thin frame kneeling in the patch of garden by the door, as if in prayer. We put our bikes inside the shed and come across, but she doesn't say a word. Just stares into the soil, her hands clasped so tight the skin across her knuckles looks set to split.

'Come inside, Mother, it's getting chilly. Shall we start on tea?'

But she doesn't hear me, is off in another place altogether. The distance is greater now, but has been part of her for as long as I can remember. Even when I was young and Kate hardly more than a baby she was this way. I'd watch her change, could tell when it was about to happen because she wouldn't answer our questions or even seem to know we were there, her eyes fixed blankly on the sky like she was a different person. But if Kate started crying, or later William, she'd return with a smile, carrying them up and becoming our mother again. The two of us would fetch flowers from the garden, because she loved to bring the colours inside: peonies with their big petals, crinkled-up carnations, and white lavender that smelled of summer alongside ragged-edged sweet williams; finally, the dahlias and Michaelmas daisies, the last to be picked.

I was sitting next to her beneath the kitchen window helping pick roses, trying not to spear my fingers on their fairy-tale thorns. A good day because the sun was bright and I had the whole summer ahead with her; I must have been about ten, I think. She knelt beside me cutting stems with a pair of rusted scissors, before placing the pink blooms into the apron draped across her lap. I garnered the loose petals, threading them together to make a necklace while she recited a poem she knew by heart. I couldn't concentrate on her words because I was arranging the colours so the darks alternated with the pales, when William started screaming out:

'Shut up, Kate. I aren't a flower. Am not!'

'Yes you are, silly billy, you're a big, pink, sweet william!'

He started chasing her around the grass – his little legs going like a partridge streaking across a field, his face all screwed and angry – but Kate was much bigger so he had no chance of catching her. Mother rose in an instant, the flowers spilling to the floor in a jagged heap, and marched over the grass to where the pair of them ran in circles.

'Stop it!' she shouted, rooting them to the spot. She came across and smacked Kate once on the backside – 'Don't tease your brother!' – then picked William up and hugged him close to calm his choking coughs.

Later, we took Father's lunch to him in one of the fields not far from home. The weather was scorching and his neck glared under the midday sun, droplets of sweat clinging to his charcoal fringe and trickling into his eyes, before he wiped them on the back of his thick forearm.

'How's my little man?' he asked, lifting the scampering, chattering William and balancing him astride his shoulders. 'And what about my three favourite girls?'

Kate sniggered as she handed him the basket wedged full of bread and cold mutton; he was smiling and his gaze lingered on Mother. I liked the way he regarded her, imagining how one day a boy would look at me that way too when we were married. With love in his eyes, I thought then, but who can tell with him? On the way back, me and Mother each held one of William's hands and swung him between us while he shrieked with little boy's laughter – a sound I've not heard for so long.

She's pushing herself up from the floor now, absently brushing the dirt from her knees. I wish we could be like that again, that she could make everything better with her smile. That pretty, wavy-haired woman who bound us all together.

My mother from another place.

7

I'm peeling the potatoes as Kate breezes down the stairs, full of sparkle as always. I can tell she has something planned because she's changed out of her pinny and looks all glamorous in her best navy skirt – the one with the permanent pleats that she got for Christmas. She leans close, like we're conspirators; Mother doesn't notice, she's prodding a cloth around the back corner by the fireplace, barely disturbing the dust from where it sleeps.

'Please come out tonight, Rachel. You deserve some fun.'

'I don't like to leave her at the minute,' I say.

But she touches me on the shoulder, imploring me with her urgent eyes. And although I've no desire to be among them all, desperately trying to be normal, hoping everything will be fine and the war will go away if they blot out the worst, I find myself unable to refuse the want in her voice. Because if the whole world is to start coming apart – if the Germans are to march across these fields any day soon – I suppose I can put up with one wasted night.

She's studying her reflection in the mirror above the fire, her eyes locked in single-minded concentration; I'll be nineteen in a few weeks and though she's only two years younger I'm an old maid in comparison. Nothing bad has ever really touched her, she's oblivious to the way things fragment before you have the chance to try and change them. It's all so clear in her head: fall for someone, move away, live happily ever after. Life never turns out like that except in stories, I want to tell her, but why spoil the illusion? Fate doesn't need me to be the bringer of bad news – it has enough ways of doing that itself.

'Come on Rachel. Please? She'll be fine. Billy'll be here with her anyway. Be good to let your hair down for once.'

I think about refusing, but know she'll wear me down in the end. 'Alright. Long as we're not back too late.'

'Thanks, it'll be a hoot!' And she gives me a peck on the cheek and starts twirling round the kitchen, getting in my way as I'm setting down the plates. I'm just dishing up as William comes in, those big hobnail boots clacking on the floor, trailing a path of mud beside.

'Take them blasted things off, Billy Abrehart!' Kate hollers at him and he smirks that grin, the same look as when he was little. 'We don't want to be cleaning up after you – me and Rachel are off out in a bit.' He's already hopping on one leg, yanking at the other foot like he's doing some Russian jig, and Kate's starting to have hysterics. Me as well, and even Mother starts to smile. Tea goes down a treat too, though there's never enough for William's wolfish appetite.

Afterwards, Mother comes across to the washing bowl but I wave her away and William takes the towel to dry while I wipe. Sometimes seeing him gives me a shock. He's beginning to look more and more like Father with the way he's shooting up, even though he's still just a boy. Only a few weeks before he finishes for summer; he might even help with the harvest this August – if he can stay out the woods for long enough. The extra money would help, but Mother won't say anything and why should I always be the ogre? He'll have to get used to working at the farm soon enough because he's only one more year of school and it'll be different after – being out with what's left of the men – than the way Miss Hexham leaves him to himself, surrounded by all them books. I worry, the way he's forever off in his little lonely world. One of these days his head might just crack open and all the things circling inside will come buzzing out, unstoppable, like a great cloud of gnats; hope no one's standing too close or they'll be deafened.

I pass him the wooden spoon – the one that's a swine to clean – with the big cleft of grease down the middle; Kate comes in from more beautifying, wearing some make-up she's dug out of nowhere.

'Got any lipstick?'

'No. There's beetroot in the cupboard if you want to use a drop of juice from that?'

'Thanks.' She turns to Mother. 'You'll be fine with Billy to-night, won't you? We're going over to see Audrey and Rose.'

But she isn't listening, standing stock-still by the table. Wouldn't surprise me to wake up one morning and find she's stopped moving altogether, so we all have to shuffle around her statue. Won't be so different, just one less place to set and one more ornament to dust. She's watching out the window up the drove again, straining for something none of the rest of us can ever make out, however hard we try.

'Let's leave the bikes. Such a nice evening.'

I wonder what she's up to. It's a fair trek and will be dark before long, and she's usually in such a hurry to get anywhere. But a walk might clear my head, so I don't bother arguing.

'If you like,' I say, as I snag closed the door. 'Where's William? He's supposed to watch Mother.'

'He won't be far. Messing about in the meadow I'd have thought.' She shouts at the top of her voice – 'Billy where you got to? Get back home!' – but I can't see him anywhere. As we start up the drove, she turns to me.

'Be fun tonight. Just us two.'

I wonder already if this is a mistake: if I should stay and make sure Mother and William are all right.

'Think he'll recognise me, Rachel?'

'Who?'

'You know. My David.'

'*Your* David?'

I thought it might be this – explains why she was so keen to come out. But I can't be bothered to listen to another load of her make-believe about a man I've never seen and she's only laid eyes on once before. Not when Tom – *my* Tom, who is real, who is flesh and blood – is stuck over there in the thick of it. How he'll cope now the fighting's finally started up is the only thing I can think about – he never was that sort, never into all that; I can't imagine him with a gun in his hand. I don't even know where he's posted but I have to find out because I couldn't bear it if...

'David – the airman from last week. Think he'll remember me?'

'How should I know? Do you have to go on, I'm not in the mood.'

'What's got you?'

'More important stuff going on in the world, if you hadn't noticed.'

I try to ignore her as we traipse away from the village and its small sounds of life. We walk either side of the grassy middle that runs along the drove, the last dregs of sunshine giving only a faint reminder of the day's earlier warmth. Chunks of earth lie strewn across the potholed surface, but at least it hasn't rained recently so my shoes shouldn't need cleaning when we get back.

'I know there's the war, but what's the point of worrying?' she says. 'We can't do anything about it. Anyway, the Colonel reckons things'll change now Mr Churchill's had a couple of weeks to settle – says he'll give the Germans a right stir.'

I don't reply, because I'm thinking of Tom: where he might be now, what he might be doing, how long before he comes home. He'll be in France somewhere, or Belgium, or one of those places, I'm sure. Wherever it is, I know the Germans won't be far away; the Colonel was reading the newspaper aloud this morning and humphing up and down in a right state about Holland falling with hardly a whimper.

'Don't reckon it'll make much odds to me if Hitler does invade. Just be working for a dictator with a different name.'

'You can be so stupid, Kate. Think about how Father got whenever anyone mentioned the last one. It'll be like that – all mud and killing – only here in front of us.'

She fixes ahead and starts fiddling with her blouse, deciding it best to stay quiet. We walk on. Out the corner of my eye a solitary poppy, which burns among the muted greenery of the verge, reminds me. That afternoon.

Our hands locked together, Tom and I made a path through the flower-strewn meadow. We arrived with hushed voices, dipping our feet into the mirrored stream as we listened to the hum of the world all around us. Finally I had to speak, had to say something to break the spell.

'Water's so cold.'

'If you follow it back it goes shallow, till it bubbles out some springs.'

He lay along the foot-worn plank that spanned the space between meadow and woods, his legs dangling either side of the makeshift bridge. I sat beside him, peering into the darkness of his face, which was cast half in shadow by the leaf-heavy branches above; watercress grew thick and wild at the sides of the narrow banks.

Now should I say it?

He raised his body and swung himself around so his thigh brushed mine and started kicking his feet, the noise masking the hiss of the breeze and the agitated chuck-chuck of a waterhen that came skimming out from the reeds, its black wings whizzing

11

like a wind-up toy. I kicked too, waves of ripples spreading out before me, their unexpectedness disturbing the placid surface. He cupped his hands together, splashing me, and I screamed at the iciness trickling down my neck.

'Tom!'

I started getting him back and soon his shirt was soaked – his rolled-up trouser legs too – but he kept hitting the wet until my hair fell in front of my face and my dress clung tight to my skin. I leant forward and gave him a shove, catching him off balance and sending him sprawling, arms aloft. He disappeared under the water and I could see him floating there beneath the surface, face down. I started to panic but then he rose, smiling, up to his waist in the stream.

'Right, that's it!' He grabbed my arm as I shrieked, and for a moment I was under too, struck dumb by the coldness. When I emerged to the air he kept on sloshing more and I lunged to-wards him, putting my arms around his neck, pressing my lips to his. And even though in that instant I knew, I still wasn't sure whether to say it. Whether it would jar the moment and make him notice the nothingness of the water. So I kept quiet. Just carried on kissing till he pulled his face away.

'Should try to get dry – get out of these wet things.' He was grinning as he spoke.

'I've nothing else...' and his mouth turned up even more as I realised what he was getting at. Now, I thought. Now should I? But I wanted him to first, so stayed silent as we waded through the water at the far side, up the bank with the grass growing dense and soft, the willow branches curtaining us like we were in one of the big four-post beds at the Hall.

'You sure?'

I nodded, catching my clumsy breath as we helped each other take off our clothes, the air thickening around us as if thunder was on the way.

'I've not...' I said, as he laid me down on the damp green, which prickled my bare skin.

'Me neither.'

Then he was inside me – at first gentle, but still I gasped – and to begin the discomfort made me uncertain what was happening before his pushing became harder. Soon I was used to the rhythmic movement of his hips, staring into his sun-caught face as he went back and forth, back and forth, thinking yes, you are the one, just like Mother told me I would know. The air around me came alive and I could hear everything merging into a sound like the sea: the whistles of the birds becoming one with the rustle of the branches. Tom's breathing shallowed and, as he grew bigger, I could sense the vibrations of thousands of tiny things moving, oblivious, inches below our sweat-drenched bodies.

'What you thinking about? It's Tom, isn't it?'

'No.'

'You ought to forget about him.' Her voice is half-obscured by the breeze, like she doesn't want me to hear. I want to scream at her – I can't forget! – my little sister with her perfect blonde waves sculpted to her head, not a hair out of place. She's just a girl anyway, doesn't know half as much as she'd like to think.

'Maybe David will have a friend there for you. Look! You've a run in your stocking.'

I turn away and ignore her mindless chatter. Better to stay silent; she can't be expected to understand. Even if I were to answer, I'm not sure the right words would come – I can barely explain it to myself.

Some things you just know.

We reach the top of the drove by the skeleton of the lightning tree. When I turn to look back our house seems tiny, squashed against the edge of the woods with only the wisp of white that rises from the chimney making it stand out from the shadows.

'Come on, we'd better get a move on,' she says. 'Reckon tonight could be the start of something.'

She heads right and begins to march in double time, her heels click-clicking on the road's surface. I fall in step, as ready as I'll ever be to sit at the side of a sweaty room watching a crowd of people get all hot and bothered.

So many fools dashing round and round the madhouse, whispering sweet nothings they'll only come to regret.

WILLIAM

Closeness smothers the half-dark. The window won't shift one inch without shattering and I have to keep the door wedged to stop them bothering me with pointless jobs. Just because the two of them are older does not mean they have the right to order me about and get on my wick the whole time.

The shed no longer smells of him, only damp soil, though he came here to get away from the women prattling around inside the house. He did not mind me being here with him, long as I stayed settled and quiet. Down among the sawdust and shavings of grey wood I watched all kinds of insects going about their lives, while he sharpened tools above: pea-bodied harvestmen bouncing along the floor, their legs too stretched for their heads; gangs of woodlice busying around the musty corners; and the brown-striped spider which strung webs between potato sacks, darting back into the shadows if I poked my stick towards its crouching fat form. I knew never to harm it, though, because he told me the rhyme:

If you want to live and thrive let a spider run alive.

I keep my collection here in some old crates. They were splintered and broken when I found them piled round the back of the farm, but I patched them up with binding twine and now they do the job just right. I line the bottoms with green moss from a fallen-over oak, which feels rough when I strip it from the trunk but soon dries soft to the touch. Almost fifty now – a lot, because every one belongs to a different kind of bird. I arrange them in rows, resting each on the padding before writing their names on paper below: the biggest egg goes in the top left, gradually getting smaller as you move across and down. Keeping them neat takes time because whenever I get a new one the rest need shifting.

Rachel and Kate moan about them taking up so much room when they come in to fetch their pushbikes. 'Least it keeps him quiet!' I heard Kate say the other morning, which had Rachel laughing as they pedalled up the drove. I do not ride his, which now stands rusting in the corner – not because it is too big, but because I prefer to use my legs: when I am out walking I can notice everything that is going on around.

The colours of the shells range from brown to blue, though most are a nearly-white. Some are plain and others covered in spots, like someone has dabbed them with a paintbrush. Quite a few are hardly bigger than a fingernail, whereas the swan's fills my palm. I thought I might lose an eye, like he warned me about, as I grabbed the egg from the nest and the cob came hissing at me, but I moved too quick for his slow, waddling strut.

Waterfowl in one crate, then field dwellers like larks and partridges in another, and two boxes of songbirds from the garden and woods. With some, like the peewit, it is hard to decide where I should put the egg because even though they stand about where water pools on the Common in winter, the nest I got its blotched-brown egg from was hidden right in among a pea crop. In the end I placed it with the field birds, but still wonder whether I was wrong and should have chosen the water box.

You should not snatch them all, he told me, else no new birds will come and the woods will fall silent. When I was little he found a hedge sparrow's neat fur-lined cup round the back of our place, tucked among the honeysuckle with five polished blue ovals wedged inside.

'Take the smallest,' he says, 'then you'll be helping them out.'

They all seem the same to me, so I cannot decide which to choose. 'Won't the parent birds be sad?'

'No, because you're getting rid of the runt, which will stop them wasting time feeding something that'll die. They'll end up having to throw an ill or weakling chick – one that's wrong – out the nest anyway, to concentrate on raising the others.'

Rachel is there with us, her face like she is going to cry. 'What if there are enough worms for all of them? You'll have stopped something growing that should be alive.'

'Wouldn't ever get bigger than a bald nestling, Rachel. Trust me. We're sparing its suffering.' He plucks one egg out and places it, all delicate, in my palm; I do not think she understands, even though she is older. Not like I do.

Now I hold the hedge sparrow's egg close to my face – that same egg that started my collection – its smooth surface almost perfect apart from the pricks in each end, which he helped me poke with a needle so I could blow out the sticky insides. All the yellow and see-through shot onto my trousers making Mother curse. Next time he will be less messy, he told her, and now I am such an expert I never get a bit down myself. I rest it back down in the box and pick out my favourite of all, which I hold to the light; he took me specially to find it – and we did too – even though it was the hardest of the lot.

We are hacking our way through the dense stuff at the back, over towards the Devil's Pit. A boy went in there once and they never did find a trace to this day. When they tried to drag it they could not reach the bottom because, they say, it goes all the way down to Hell.

We get to where the briers are snarled the worst and it is a struggle to twist through the thorny branches. He turns to me, pressing his finger to his lips and signalling to be quiet. He points, but at first I cannot spot a thing.

'What?' I mouth and he lifts me up, because I must be no more than seven or eight.

'There.'

From higher, I can see it in a gap on the ground: a scruffy cup of dead leaves with two pale, blue-green eggs inside, resting on a cushion of down.

'A magic piper laid them,' he whispers, and at that moment a rich fluting bubbles up around us. We go towards the sound – me snagging my sleeve on a bramble – but always the player somewhere in front of us, out of sight.

Not magic, I know now, only a nightingale.

I am done, so cover the collection with sackcloth to stop the eggs from spoiling, padding it down, careful as anything, on top of each box. A breath of cool blasts my head when I shove the door with my foot, a shock after the stuffiness of the shed. Outside, the growing shadows suck me into their silence, and I know where I must go. Moving sharply, I head towards his new place, tucked between the fields where he worked and took me walking.

I suppose, at least, he must be grateful for the stillness.

16

A mottled-brown blackbird eyes me with suspicion from beneath the headless angel's smooth stump. It moves in bursts between the graves, speckled and dirty with eyes too big for its face – an early young one not long out of the nest. Did it fall before time, because its wings look short and weak like it has not yet learned to fly? It will not be safe on the ground with all the cats and stoats around, and I cannot spot the parent birds anywhere. Straining upright, only a few feet from where I sit, it tilts its head at me, its beak open like it wants to whistle for help. I cup my hands together and edge them towards its puffed-out body; I will take it home to care for and raise myself. Rachel will not approve – she hates any extra bother or mess – but I can keep it secret in the shed and bring it worms to eat.

Now the fledgling hops closer, inches from my upturned palms; I grab forward and it skitters away, half-running, half-gliding till it takes to the air, landing clumsily on top of the tall stone cross, a memorial to the men from round here that died in the last war. The fighting he was in.

This one has been going since September but hardly nothing has happened till two weeks ago when the Germans started this way: now people are looking grey-faced, talking about how it is all going to go off any day soon.

I try again to think back to him and me before; I am almost at remembering when a huffing down the path disturbs the quiet. I adjust my position and see Mrs Heckleton coming, so slump into the spongy grass where I can watch in secret. Look at her strutting among the headstones, like someone has put her in charge of the place. All she does is delve into everyone else's misery, rubbing it in their faces, because she is in love with death. Scratting about on her hands and knees, she stoops beside an oblong stone. Her scrunched-up features sag, and she starts pulling ancient daffodils from a vase. 'Well Harold,' she talk-whispers, 'it's not been too bad a day.'

I realise she is jawing out loud to someone below – her Dearly Departed. He will not reply, you silly old cow, I want to shout, though I suppose I know why she does it. Not that I come expecting any answers, with me up here and him wedged into that smooth-planed box. Those times when him and me would go

17

about together are never coming back, even though they appear like pictures in front of my eyes. Almost as clear as being there.

We are in the heart of the winter-stripped woods: the brambles have lost their bite and the nettles have shrunk to nothing because of the frost. My stick clears a good path in front of me; it takes no effort with so little life left in the ground.

'Not so loud, William. You're not beating at a shoot.'

I stop whacking over the dried-up stems and try to step, noiseless, through the drifts of brittle leaves, like the way he does.

'When we get home, don't say anything to your mother 'bout what we've been up to.'

'Why?'

'She'll only worry and get all flustered. Don't go telling anyone else either.'

'Would they mind too?'

'They might think we've been doing something we shouldn't. Trespassing. Because we don't own the pheasants.'

'Who does then?'

'The Colonel, I suppose. But he's got plenty – he won't miss one.'

I concentrate so as not to crunch any twigs, but it is impossible and I cause a loud snap which makes him turn and give me a pretend angry look that is really a smile. We carry on; another crack and a jarring whirr of wings as a brown hen pheasant gets up from under my toes. I jump back and he is laughing.

'Noisy buggers, aren't they?'

'Why didn't you get it?'

'Too quick once they've taken off. Besides, I want a nice fat male.'

I step across the rickety plank that has been shoved over the brook below; immediately we are into a place where thicker trees stop the light reaching all the way to the ground. My waterboots squelch through greedy pockets of mud, which try to swallow my feet.

'Have I ever told you what happened here?' he asks, and I shake my head.

'No.'

'This wood is haunted.'

I am quiet, my footsteps falling in with his, because I love it when he tells me a story. I move quickly to keep up as we trudge ever onwards.

'A long time ago a brother and a sister, little more than babies, lived in the big Hall where your sisters work. They grew up happy, because their parents were good people and full of wealth. But sadness struck, as first the mother, then the father, caught a fever they couldn't shake. Their uncle promised he'd care for the children after they'd gone, but already his mind was set on the Hall and its land, which he wanted for himself.'

'What were they sick with?'

'I don't know – a bad fever like people got in them days. Anyway, the parents passed and the uncle came to the Hall. But living there was a constant reminder to him that it would all belong to the children when they were old enough. So he hatched a plan to get rid of them, so everything could become his. He hired two soldiers from his time fighting abroad to do away with them secretly in this very wood, knowing their bodies would never be found, what with how thick it is.'

The darkness does not let up as we tramp on and I hardly care about my aching legs because I am listening so hard to every single word he is saying.

'The men snatched the brother and sister as they played in the grounds of the Hall, bringing them to the wood as instructed. Once under the tangle of trees, the sunlight dwindled and the leaves began to whisper. One of them, a scoundrel with a bushy black beard, decided he could not stomach to kill the boy wriggling around in the sack that was slung on his back. So he said to the other...'

'What did he look like?'

'I don't... He was a thin, wiry man.' He grins. 'A bit like Mr Marsham.'

I giggle and he pauses, spitting out a big wedge of gob to clear his throat. 'Anyway, he said to the other: "Why don't we just leave them here? We already have our money, there's no need to do away with the little ones." But the thin man had been turned by the horrors he'd seen on the battlefield and a killing-feeling was rising inside him once more.'

'Did you see things like that when you were in the war?'

19

He goes quiet and all I can hear is the swish of our feet trailing through the mulch of leaves and muck that suffocates the floor.

'What was the worst?' I ask, breaking the stillness.

'Don't you want the rest of this story? We're in the middle of the wood now, right where it happened!'

'Please,' I say. 'Sorry.'

'Well... The wiry one refused to spare them and a fight broke out in which he was stabbed straight through his heart. Then the bearded man cut open the sacks and let the children out, telling them to wait and he would soon bring them food. Instead, he went off counting his money, reaching an inn just before night-fall where he drank himself to a stupor. When he woke the next day, all thoughts of going back had gone. The two little ones were alone and petrified. It was too thick in the wood for them to move far, so they stayed put, huddling together for warmth and singing nursery songs to keep their spirits up.'

'I wouldn't have been scared in here in the dark.'

'No?' He is grinning. 'Are you sure? Because they were, the poor things. But they made it through to the next morning, expecting the man to appear any moment in the dawn light. Only he didn't, and they had to keep waiting.'

'Why didn't they try to get out?'

'They were much smaller than you. Babies really. And they weren't used to going about the woods like you do with me, so they didn't move an inch. But as the day wore on and the man failed to return again, their strength faded. After a further night they joined their parents in that other place, succumbing because of the man's selfishness. A robin redbreast found them, cradled in each other's arms. He flittered above them, singing a mourn-ful song as he covered their tiny bodies with leaves.'

'They died?'

'Yes.'

As we walk on no robins call from the branches around us – it is winter and all the birds are quiet: too busy searching for the last of the berries, or the tiny worms that do not stray far below the surface.

'Months later in a distant town, the bearded man was caught committing some other crime.'

'What?'

'Robbing or something, it doesn't matter – what he did isn't part of the story.'

I nod, sorry that I have interrupted him because I can tell from his face that he is getting to the main bit.

'As he was about to be hanged he begged forgiveness for his part in the disappearance of the two little ones, confessing how he'd been paid to do what had happened. News got back to the village and an angry party went out, but the uncle got word first and fled here to hide. Once underneath the black canopy he heard strange voices and cowered inside a gouged-out oak so as not to have to listen to the terrible things they whispered to him.'

'Whereabouts is it?' I say, excited and scared. 'Can we go look?'

'Used to be round here, but I don't think it's still standing. This would have been the place though – the oldest, darkest part of the wood.'

I shiver and hold out my hand, which he swamps in his.

'The villagers came in after him. The robin flew ahead, leading them first to the fox-picked bones of the wiry man, then the leaf-strewn bodies of the two children, who lay peaceful and pre-served, like newborn babies asleep in their cots. The bird flew on towards the heart of the wood and perched on the ancient tree, singing his sad song once more. The villagers followed and, hear-ing whimpering inside, discovered the uncle's hiding place. They lugged him out and revenged the niece and nephew by hanging him from a rope thrown over one of the oak's thick boughs.'

'What happened?'

'His neck snapped easy as anything, his legs kicked out, and his body jarred and jerked.'

I shudder at the thought. 'What about the little ones?'

'They say you can sometimes catch sight of them hand-in-hand as they flash through the wood before you in the late af-ternoon light.'

I grip his fingers tight.

'Don't worry,' he says, 'I've never seen them yet.'

We are coming out of the gloom; the trees are less gnarled, and slim saplings fight for the sunlight.

'Shush. Over there.'

In the clearing stands a cock pheasant: burgundy and green and iridescent, its collar white like the Reverend's as it scuffs among the undergrowth. He lets go of my hand and pulls back on his catapult. The rounded stone flies straight into the side of the bird, sending it sprawling in a cascade of feathers. He springs across, pouncing onto it like a cat. Holding its panting, scared body to his face for a closer look, he breaks its neck with a sharp twist.

'We'll tell your mother we just found it lying about.'

As we walk home – him carrying the pheasant's flopping carcass so that its tail becomes kinked and coated with mud – he asks me to repeat his story. And as I do he is right: it feels like the children are crouching there beside us as my words float about the trees, which in turn lower their branches to listen.

I forget where I am for a second and stretch out my arms. Mrs Heckleton turns from where she has been talking to her husband and, noticing me for the first time, makes a whelp like a scared terrier.

'Tell it back, William.' That is what he said to me. 'Speaking it aloud means your tongue will always remember.'

I rise, my legs awkward from kneeling, and stare down at his sticks, wondering whether the opposite is true: if not saying will make it all come apart, untethering my memories to canter away like stray horses.

Because, even though I must try to remember everything we ever did together, there are some times I would rather forget.

MRS HECKLETON

I've almost finished talking with Harold when I sense someone's gaze burrowing into my very soul. I turn to find that boy squatting there among the gloom of the graves, twiddling a blade of grass between his fingers, quite content with himself. Been watching me in secret the whole time.

'What you trying to do, William Abrehart, frighten an old woman half to death?'

He gave me such a start, coming out of nothing so I didn't catch a single step. It's no surprise he's that way when you look at the rest of them, though it can't have been easy for Louise with everything what's happened. My heart goes out to the poor woman, barely able to cope, while that pair of little madams gad about like not a thing's amiss. Perhaps they're still too young to understand, but one day they'll wake up and it'll hit them. Even so, how they've left that man to lie there, all anonymous, is plain disrespectful to his memory as a father and husband; I know they've never had much, but don't remember anything proper marking out their final reposes, just sorry wooden crosses and wilting flowers that are forgotten as soon as they're laid. These crooked twigs take a bit of beating though – however many excuses I make for what they've been through, that isn't right: a family should show some dignity and respect, even if they never have been gravestone people. You can walk round this churchyard and read the chiselled names of plenty of my lot, and it's not like we ever had two ha'pennies to rub together either.

He keeps scowling at me as I hoist myself to my feet.

'What you gawking at?' I snap, though really, what's the point? I thought this phase would pass and he'd have tired of it after a whole year, but it seems to have stuck. Funny, when you think about it. Because even people away over the Common swear they could hear the din that boy made as his father was lowered into the very ground he now squats so stubbornly above.

Was a big turnout – most of the village, and plenty more besides, including the Colonel. The Reverend gave a lovely service, almost bringing a tear to my eye when he told how sorely John Abrehart would be missed. I know I wasn't alone in sitting there dabbing a hankie, you only had to look around to see all the women welling up; though when the Reverend went on to describe what a generous man the deceased had been – happy to share everything with his neighbours – I don't think he intended what some of us might have been thinking. Funerals aren't a time for uncharitable thoughts, but when a person has tried to live their life the right way, like I always have, you can't just switch a feeling off because the occasion doesn't suit.

All said, though, it was as bright a morning as you could have wished for, at least until William started up. Now I know a lad's allowed to grieve the passing of his father – and it can't have been easy as he was the one who found him in such queer circumstances – but Rachel or Kate should have shaken or slapped him, because they were all squashed in together in the tall box pew at the front. None of us could see who was making the racket, but we knew. We'd got as far as *Fast falls the eventide* when he erupted. Irene Johnson gamely kept going on the organ and some of us tried our best to drown it, but after struggling on to the *Change and decay*, we petered out and were left listening to the lad's hysterics, shouting and screaming like a creature possessed.

Eventually Jack Earl fetched him away so the Reverend could continue, but he kept carrying on in the graveyard. He was still yawping as we went outside and the noise only got worse when they started letting down the coffin. Jack said later it took all of his strength to restrain him, and him being a big man too. I hate to think what might've happened if he hadn't. Wouldn't have surprised me to watch the boy follow his father into that hole, such was the wild expression about his face.

You can't tell looking at him now, though. Must have used all his voice up right there and then, because he hasn't uttered a single word to a living soul since. Not even his poor dear mother.

No, that day couldn't have been more different to the one a couple of months before: the five of them huddled at the front, with only me and Lily Morley tucked into the shadows at the back. Such a silent affair. Eerie almost. Maybe I shouldn't have gone, but I told myself, Betty you've not missed a person being put to rest in this church in over forty years, and just because circumstances aren't

24

regular doesn't mean you should start now. If you're not present to bear witness who will be, other than the Reverend?

And Him up there, of course – for we all know how He cares for the little ones the deepest.

RACHEL

The air's sweating and they're spinning like tops; I can hardly breathe because the sight of all these soldiers and pilots in their uniforms reminds me: Tom enjoyed a dance as much as the next man, once he came out of himself and shed his shyness. Only we never got to many together, because everything came too quick. Not that it matters now, what we had was worth a thousand nights like this.

'Rachel!'

Kate and her airman are back inside the room. She peels off from him, stepping clumsily through the crowd and half-falling onto the bench beside me, her face flushed, her lipstick a mess.

'Your blouse is out. Ought to be careful you don't get a reputation,' I say.

'Maybe I want one.'

I turn away. She's too tipsy to see she's making a fool of herself. Now he's coming over, a pint in one hand and two little glasses looking silly in the other.

'Here you go. Two port and lemons. Mind if I sit? All that dancing's done me in!' He takes a big swig of beer and plants himself between us. Kate snatches her glass greedily and starts sipping the port as he turns to me.

'David,' he says. 'Corporal David Carter, four three six seven eight, at your service!'

'I know.'

My reply throws him and I can tell he can't think what to say. Kate is giggling; she's slipped her hand onto his knee and is leaning her head on his shoulder. Her drink's already gone and now she's trying to grab my glass. I let her take it and rise unsteadily – the closeness of the air and all the movement in the room is making me queasy.

'Excuse me,' I say, a haze fogging my head as I blunder across the dance floor, into the shock of the night. I gulp lungfuls of cold air and hurry round the corner to clear my head. A couple slink from the side of the building, the girl fiddling with her dress and the soldier fumbling in his pocket; I can't remember her name, though I recognise her from around – I think she's from Norwich, sent over to stay with her aunt. They snigger as they stride past me; I keep on ahead, surrendering to the calm cool of the dark.

Kate's eyes flicker open.

'Oh it's you, Rachel. Was wondering where'd you got to.'

'Getting some air. I feel better now.'

'David's not like lads from round here, is he?' Can you believe it, me and an RAF man!'

'Suppose not.'

'How tall must he be? Six foot easy! His talk's so different too. And he's such a gentleman, isn't he?'

Even in the room's half-light my sister's face looks flustered. A stray clump of blonde hair trails across her mouth, sticking like a cobweb to her lips. David is fetching another drink, though we should get going because she's had far too much already.

'When the war's finished I can picture me and him walking arm in arm along one of those posh London streets, looking in all the lah-di-dah shop windows and eating sandwiches in some fancy café. You, Mother and William can come visit.'

The music's gone up a notch and it's hard to concentrate on what she's saying, because her words are slow and slurred, like sleeptalking almost.

'Hands so soft, can tell he's never worked the land. He's a wonderful kisser, Rachel.'

The dancers circle faster and faster, their arms and legs flailing the air as the last of my drink burns my throat. He returns with more and I watch Kate's fingers brush the coarse fabric of his trousers. She leans in and rests her head on his shoulder again, but he doesn't move an inch as he talks to me.

'You sure you two are sisters?' he asks, a grin spreading across his face.

'Course we are. Why?'

'You're so different, that's all. You with your dark hair and your sister so fair.'

I shrug.

'So what are your plans? What will you do when it's all over?' he says.

'Plans? I haven't. There's Mother and William to look after.'

'Your brother?'

I nod.

'You can't put it all on hold for them though, can you? Got to live your own life.'

I find myself smirking at all his talk – even if I could leave I wouldn't want to because how would Tom know where to find me if I'd gone? For a moment I want to tell him everything, share my secrets with this stranger, but the drink and the noise, and the mugginess of the room keeps me tongue-tied. A part of me is flattered he's showing so much interest, like I am a real person and not just some servant at the Hall, but I still want to change the subject.

'What schemes you hatching then?'

'Best not to think too far ahead in this line of work,' he smiles, pointing at the stripes on his arm. Kate has slumped against him, dead to the world. 'Suppose I'll go and help the old man with the carpentry. Reckons he'll retire in a few years and leave me in charge of the yard.'

'You'll land on your feet.'

'Wish I had your confidence – landing's part of the problem. We lost another crew Tuesday night.'

Now his eyes are scared and he no longer seems as confident, as sophisticated, as I first thought. He can't be that much older than me, I think, yet he's way up there in the sky each night, not sure whether he'll make it from one day to the next. Like Tom, who this minute must be right among it, crouched in a bunker ready to hold back the Germans when they come marching his way. For a second I want to reach my hand across and touch the face of this man – this boy, really – to let him know it's not wrong to be frightened. But I'm saved from offering any false comfort as Kate starts squirming and giggling – 'David, I've finished my drink!' – and the moment passes.

The night's got a nip so he wraps his jacket across my sister's shoulders.

'You're such a gentleman, David. Knew you'd walk me home!' She slurs out her words and now I realise why she didn't want to bring the bikes – she can be such a sly one. She's leaning against him, wobbling all over the place, so I prop myself against her other side, putting my arm around her waist, and we start back. Away from the noise of the dance and the smell of sweat and spilled beer it feels awkward and neither David nor I make a sound, though Kate is singing and chattering so loud I worry she'll wake the whole village.

'Quieten down!' I snap, and she settles a little, still blathering in whispers to David, making no particular sense.

We return in what seems like no time – though it must be a good half-hour walk – and I pull her towards the front door. She giggles, her finger pressed to her lips, miming silence. A curtain twitches up in Billy's room, but falls quickly back.

'Thanks for helping get her home,' I say to David. 'Sorry she's got so tipsy.'

'I'm not tipsy!'

'Don't mention it. Maybe the three of us can do this again... Go dancing or something, I mean.'

'She'd love to, I'm sure,' I mutter and he stands there grinning. 'Night then,' I say, embarrassed at the sound of my echoing voice in the middle of all the nothing.

'David!' Kate stumbles against him, reaching up to his face. He seems unsure what to do with her and I have to about drag her away, her hands still pawing the empty air as I open the door. Inside, we fumble in the shadows – like the blind – trying not to wake Mother. I try to shepherd my little sister through the kitchen and up the stairs but she stands frozen, staring at the floor.

'Got to go to him,' she says. Her face looks shattered.

'Not now. You'll see him again soon enough.'

'But I don't want to become a statue like you and Mother.'

'Come on, you're drunk. Let's get you to bed.'

'I can still catch him up. I've got to get away, Rachel.'

She seems utterly lost and I think I understand: this place is too small for her; she should be out living her life in the bigger world while she's still got a chance. At the same time I'm filled with the conviction I must remain, despite what David was saying about plans and the future and all that nonsense. Because, when he returns from abroad, this is the place where Tom and I will make everything better.

29

We pass the kitchen window and I can see David loitering at the end of the garden. Kate notices too and flops against me for support. I push her on, guiding her up the stairs to her bed, where she collapses into an instant sleep, her mouth half-open like she's about to say something of vital importance. I pull off her shoes and cover her with the blanket before nestling beside her, stroking stray hairs from her sweat-washed forehead.

When I rise the room is skewed and I stagger, shaking, onto my own bed; I only drank two glasses and should be fine but my head has started to spin furiously and everything is happening all at once. I lie back and Tom's perfect face waltzes around the dark space, like the dancers in the hall. I have to see him again, I really do, because things should not have been left that way between us. Why couldn't he have come back when I needed him most? He should've. That one time, at least. He should have.

Kate mutters something from her slumber – I can't understand what she is trying to say – before exhaling the deepest of sighs. The interruption causes Tom's face to vanish abruptly from my head, but it doesn't matter now.

Because I will wait for him as long as it takes.

WILLIAM

Even in the middle of the day the corridor leading to his room is a tunnel. When I was small I was scared to walk its blackness, especially if I had been dreaming bad. But only him or Mother could make the night-people go from my head, so I had to feel my way those few shadowed steps, running my fingers along the bone-smooth walls. Inside they would be fast off: her on her back, hands clasped above the blanket; him with his bare arms and legs flung outside the sheets. Some evenings, if I wake, I can hear her stirring; she cannot sleep hardly at all, which must be why she always seems so tired. She has her candle lit tonight – the door is framed by a flickering halo though the sun has long been set.

Rachel calls it Mother's room, which is not right, because before it was his. When do we cease to possess the things that once, without question, belonged to us? When I found him, was the room already hers? Later, at the exact moment the mechanical rise and fall of his chest subsided? Or do his teeth and bones – the very last of him to remain – cling to ownership even now?

Earlier I fetched his jacket from the wardrobe, sneaking in when Mother was downstairs so as not to upset her. I check my door is pulled tight, and begin to imagine myself as him, standing rigid in front of the mirror to see if I look the same. Rachel and me share his dark hair and eyes, and Kate says I have the Abrehart nose. Not huge, like the Reverend's red-tipped hooter, yet not small either – it has something of the bill of a hawk, which is good. I study the reflection within the shade-filled glass, but the face staring back is still my own, so I dip my fingers into the cup of water by the bed and run them through my hair, brushing it the same way as him. It is no good, though, the likeness is no closer – the jacket is too big and the sleeves hang way down, as if I have no hands.

I empty the jacket pockets onto the floor so I can see and feel his things: the big white handkerchief, a few pennies, his comb; his catapult too, which he took when we went walking, for the pheasants and rabbits. My favourite is his best knife, the one he always carries. The blade folds into the smooth bone handle and is so sharp that if your finger skims the metal for only a second a dark line appears. I think about touching it, but know what will happen so stop myself. I wanted to place them all with him in the box but they fastened down the lid before I could. That was BLOODY WRONG – they are his things and should be next to him – even though part of me is glad I still have them here to look at. And to touch.

I hold the jacket tight to my nose and inhale, pressing hard against the cloth so the mix of sweat and dirt he brings home from the farm surrounds me again. I breathe him in until the tears and snot flood my face, screwing my eyes shut so I can concentrate and remember. Because I do not want it ever to be different.

Like me and him up by the Black Sheds, our thin poles of ash casting worms into the water, which is at once dark and dazzling where the sun has found a way through the curtain of oak leaves above. I glance over and he is intent, staring at a shimmer among the swaying weeds, a razor of light making his coal-black hair glisten. He stands tall like a harnser, his eyes focussed only on the beck below. Suddenly he strikes and we are onto an unending shoal. For the next few minutes – though it seems hours – we pull wriggling silver sticks from the cold wet, each transforming into a gulping, dying roach when we lay them on the bank.

'Look at the fins, William,' he says. 'Like blood. Red, like blood.'

My sisters have gone to meet Audrey and Rose in Summer End. Audrey is seventeen, like Kate, but Rose is prettier and two years closer to me. Kate is always teasing me about her, asking whether I have kissed a girl yet. When I storm off she laughs and asks if I am keen on Miss Hexham instead, and my face flushes because that is not the case. She is my teacher, that is all, and she gives me books and poems to read. At the moment it is Charles Dickens's *Great Expectations*, which is about a murderer let loose among the mist and marshes. Exciting stuff, though if I had been the boy I would not have brought food to the prisoner but left him there to starve. Besides, Kate says Miss Hexham has a secret sweetheart over in France and the other morning I could see she looked close to welling up as we prayed for all the brave soldiers, sailors and air men risking their lives for this country.

He quizzed me too, the last time he took me berrying on the Common. But it was different, because he was not teasing like

Kate, only interested. The room's night-quiet helps me make a head-picture, and the sound of his voice comes right away, for once, as if he is standing against me in the dark.

'Remind me how old you are,' he says, reaching up and dropping the sloes into the patched-up tin bucket. The first frost came in the night so they are ready for picking, no longer tasting as cloudy and sour.

'Eleven.'

He is smirking at me.

'Wouldn't mind being that age again – must've been about when I had my first proper kiss. How about you? You kissed a girl yet?'

I feel my face flushing but say nothing.

'My first time was coming home from school – Mary she was. Mary Howard. We got caught in the rain so ran inside a barn to shelter. As we waited I leant over and kissed her on the cheek.'

I am embarrassed and concentrate on how I will soon be helping him to pierce each berry, pressing them down in the big jars so he can make the deep-red gin he drinks sometimes of an evening. Once he let me have a mouthful, which rusted my throat and made my face burn.

'Must be someone you've took a fancy to?'

I do not answer but stare into the greyness.

'Take my advice – don't try too hard and they'll come to you. Shouldn't worry about the rest.'

'What about Mother,' I say, 'when did you first kiss her?'

'Let's think... A couple of weeks after we met. She was showing me the house where I was born – the one in the woods that's not safe to go in no more – we had to brush through the hanging ivy to get inside. That's when. Not long after I'd come back from abroad.'

I rise from bed and peer behind the curtain. The moon is gibbous and gives the garden a silver-grey glow. When I am old enough for the army I will join up like he did. I have the brass tin him and all the soldiers were given at Christmas during the fighting by Princess Mary. Back then it was filled with cigarettes; now I keep two photographs inside: one of him as a soldier and another of Grandfather Sampson who I cannot remember, though everyone says was a good man. He was in the Great War and worked on the farm too, but there was an accident when I was a baby and a horse put a hoof in his head. That is why I do not trust horses – they are not like cattle, which you can clap or shout at to scare back. A horse might scuttle off or, if the mood takes it, just as easy rear up at you.

There are fewer at the farm now they have the tractor and I hope I do not have much to do with them when I start work there. Mr Croxton said it is good that Mr Marsham, who is the Estate Manager, has said he will take me on when I finish at school, as I would find another job hard to come by with what he calls my propensity for silence. He also tells us, when he is giving his headmaster talk each morning, that this war could go on even longer than the last, and will be a tremendous struggle with many sacrifices to be made. 'ENGLAND WILL PREVAIL!' he shouts, his words all loud and wobbly. The Germans, he says, are either at your feet or at your throat, and like before will not have the stomach when things get going. Not when they meet our men, fighting like hell. We can do our bit too by having our wits about us at all times and keeping an eye out for anything suspicious, because they have already got their filthy spies milling around the countryside disguised as nuns, and even blind men with sticks who can see perfectly – digging out information in advance of their invasion.

A movement along the drove makes me concentrate, alert. Three figures emerge from the gloom and, as they reach the edge of the garden, I can make out it is Rachel and Kate alongside a tall man in dark clothes. Kate is leaning against him, her arm clamped round his waist. They are crossing the grass and now I realise he is wearing a uniform. I think for a moment he might be a German come already, but then I see he is one of ours.

He is an air man.

Kate is giggling and trying to kiss him and I want to shout at her to STOP – because I must keep my word – and he would not have wanted them being out this much past dark. Especially with a soldier or air man.

Not after what happened before.

34

Rachel glances at my window; I lean back and let the curtain fall to. She must not realise I know, but I will make sure they are safe and follow them in future, even though the pair of them craze me with the way they go on. Because I said to him that I would be the man, as we were against the stairs, the dying light pouring through the doorway.

'Look after your mother and your sisters,' he rasped, though his eyes were dark and scared as I promised him I would.

Promised him I would.

MOTHER

Empty voices reverberate round the dark wooden beams that criss-cross the ceiling of the church. Louise Abrehart is floating above herself, staring down at a woman who looks so much older than her forty years: grey hair, grey skin, grey circles beneath her eyes.

Time is indeterminable; the days bleed into one. Like when she was a girl helping Nan to make chutney – stirring the vinegar, sugar and tomatoes for an eternity, till everything had coalesced to the old lady's satisfaction. Now there is no one to tell her when things are ready and Louise misses that. Misses Nan too: big and soft with roasted cheeks and kind eyes, her white hair buried beneath a beret and her sleeves around her elbows, forever busying herself with something.

'Such a dreamer, my girl!' she says. 'Always got your head in a book.'

Louise sits at the kitchen table alongside Nan and Mother, who are shelling broad beans, the tips of their fingers black as they extract the fat seeds and toss them towards the cracked blue-and-white bowl. Her eyes only half-follow their actions, concentrating instead on the poem she is reading, which spins her mind into the silence of the moonlit woods, despite the steady chatter of the two older women and the sunshine that is streaming through the window.

Is there anybody there? Is there?

Only that awkward man peering over me, his hands trembling against the carved wood as he speaks:

'For this people's heart is waxed gross, their ears are dull of hearing, and their eyes they have closed; lest at any time they should see with their eyes and hear with their ears, and should understand with their heart, and should be converted. And I should heal them.'

His silhouette looms over us and now I remember: the Reverend. Sunday morning; I am in church.

'But blessed are your eyes, for they see. And your ears, for they hear. For I say unto you that many prophets and righteous men have desired to see those things which you see, and have not seen them; and to hear those things which you hear, and have not heard them.'

I yearn to find meaning among his words, but they make no sense – just a jumble of sounds that talk a hole through my head – and I can feel the ice-white harshness that pours through the windows, like light inside a glasshouse, mesmerising me, and I cannot stop myself from becoming Not-Louise again: that flitting stranger who inhabits my form.

The hoar-crusted hedge lining the drove as she emerges, shivering, into the garden from the privy reminds Louise of a poem she learnt by rote at school:

'The Frost performs its secret ministry, Unhelped by any wind.'
Samuel Taylor Coleridge, she remembers.

The air stirs at the edge of her sight. Like heat haze at first, but it can't be on a morning so cold. The shape takes form as she stands, spellbound, stamping on the spot to keep warm. Her dragon's breath sends clouds in front of her face, adding to the illusion of the approaching outline, still a mystery until she realises it is a figure on a bicycle. Who'd be about at this time on such an icy, cobwebbed morning? Her feet rupture the perfection of the ground's white-bladed rind, and now she can make out a tall man teetering on a metal frame that seems too fragile to hold his strapping bulk.

A soldier in green uniform and cap.

His approach is a struggle, his breathing hard fog. He's close now, watching the road with violent concentration, before veering onto the embankment at the garden's edge. He makes towards her, losing control and ploughing into the hedge in a tangle of limbs and bicycle. She rushes over and he gives a sheepish grin, which means thankfully he is not hurt. Giggles explode from her mouth in puffs of steam as she offers him her hand. He takes it, and she is struck by the cleanness of his fingernails.

'Thank you, miss,' and her cheeks redden, the cold forgotten. His cap has fallen and she bends to pluck it from the crisp, frosted grass, mesmerised by his tar-black head of hair.

'I'm looking for Albert Sampson. Would you know where I could find him?' he asks, brushing the rime and crystallized

leaves off his jacket. She can't take her gaze from his face, until his smile shakes her from the trance.

'Sorry, I didn't mean to... Albert Sampson's my father. Why don't you come out the cold?'

And the man whose name she doesn't yet know is crunching over the grass beside her, his bicycle abandoned to the hedge. Inside she learns that this is the hero who served alongside Albert Sampson in the 8th Battalion of the Norfolks, the pair of them somehow overcoming the terror and blood of those dirt-coated months; a time she knows her father cannot bear to think about, let alone talk of, except to say he owed his life to a brave lad who dragged him from the quagmire of the Somme and fought with him right through the rest of the war.

'John Abrehart! My good luck charm. Pure-bottled luck!' her father exclaims, happier than she's seen him in the weeks and months since he's been home. Mother and Nan rise in awe of this saviour in their midst, urging him to sit down by the fire, taking the best cups from the pantry and shoving thick slices of bread onto toasting forks.

'What brings you here, Mr Abrehart?' Louise asks above the laughter when he is seated, and he stares back at her with such intensity she has to look down at her shoes, which now she notices, embarrassed, are all scuffed and scratched.

'Well, miss. Albert – I mean your father – said if we should both make it home in one piece from old Fritz, that if I should ever need work to come find him and he'll have a word in the Colonel's ear. Because the Estate could always do with a good pair of extra hands.'

'We'll see you right, John,' her father is saying. 'Won't have to wear that uniform no more, neither!'

'Can't get used to nothing else – keep putting it on out of habit. Was lying in bed, trying to get back to sleep, when I re-membered your words and thought no time like the present – hadn't realised how early it was till I got going. No one about this time on a Sunday!'

Nan pipes up, forgetting the bread, which is starting to char.

'You're not to do with Wesley Abrehart, the keeper here a few years back, are you?' She stops mid-sentence, her chuckling abruptly subsiding.

38

'Yes.' He pauses for longer than the room seems comfortable with, before continuing. 'Yes. He was my father, as I told Albert – Mr Sampson – in the trenches. Mother says we lived here till I was four, though I don't hardly remember. We moved the other side of Swaffham with my uncle and aunt soon after. After Father.'

'Well, it was a shock to us all.' Nan's face looks solemn. 'I can still picture you as a little old boy running about all over the place. Course, the house where you were born isn't lived in any more. Not since.'

The old lady suddenly notices the blackened toast and pulls the fork from the fire, dull flames snatching up at her fingers as her face softens to a smile.

One week on and John Abrehart is living with them. Louise is happy to make way and share a room with Nan, putting up with her snoring and sleep-talk to be near this handsome man with midnight hair. Back from the Hall each evening, she sits in the corner looking over at John when she thinks his attention is focussed elsewhere. Sometimes he catches her stare and smiles in silent reply. This is how it starts to happen, how she comes to be with the man who saved her father from the trenches and the mud.

Four months on and she is walking up the aisle, the noonday sun illuminating the borrowed white dress she really has no right to wear, but her father has insisted: 'To hell with what people might think. You're not the first – nor the last – and you won't find a finer lad!'

And he's right, it doesn't seem to matter because even the heavens are shining down on her wedding day. Nan and Mother stand with smiles so wide, Father prouder than ever as he escorts her to the altar and the waiting John Abrehart. As she repeats the words, she can picture how perfect her life will be from this point forward with her war-hero husband.

Always for the better, she thinks, never for the worse.

Always John Abrehart and his pure-bottled luck.

'All rise for Number 165 in your hymnals.'

The Reverend's instruction, and Rachel's gentle tapping on my arm, brings me back into myself. I should join with their hymn, raise my small voice to the heavens, but the drone of the organ is already taking me again, pulling me into that scarlet night.

'Time, like an ever-rolling stream, bears all its sons away...'

I feel it starting, but I will not succumb. Not here. I will not enter the reddening, where it all becomes tainted, and the ill luck takes hold among the shouting and the blur. Afterwards everything sliding away so much faster than it should and then Nan gone too; Mother three months later, a lump the size of an orange in her breast; finally, Father and the horse – a real tragedy for the Estate said the Colonel.

I cling to my hymn book. Rachel's sweet voice binds my feet to the floor of the church, as a momentary tightness jabs my chest. William's stooped shoulders are turned to me, his arms pumping the bellows of the organ as if his very being depends on it. Don't rest for a minute, my silent one, because if you do the ill luck will creep close, and once it starts there's no stopping, such is the speed it gathers. Everything unravels and all the hollowness opens up till there is nothing left. Only shame-filled flowers.

'Our hope for years to come.'

They are singing the last verse, a repeat of the first, though this time I hear the words themselves and not just the sounds their mouths make. Now the noise subsides and a different one begins to rumble around me: the Lord's Prayer. I unhook the tattered red cushion from the pew in front, laying it down and lowering myself. As my knees press into the worn cloth, the forbidden word pops from my mouth before I can stop it. Too late for the hymn that has ended, but I do not care.

'Hope.' Mine alone, never ours.

My Hope. For years to come.

WILLIAM

Our Father, who art in the ground,
Hollow be thy grave.
Thy kingdom come.
Thy William done on earth,
As you made him promise.
Give us this day our daily bread
And forgive us our trespassing
(But forgive not those who trespass against us).
Lead my sisters not into temptation,
But deliver them from evil.
For thine is the kingdom,
The power, and the glory,
For ever and ever
Abrehart.

The Reverend rumbles on. May the blessing and all that. Get on with it, there are better places to be of a May morning than this cobwebbed palace with its high windows: outside the hedges are noisy with whitethroats scratching out their songs and turtle doves purring like well-fed cats.

At last, his lips stop moving and he fidgets his hands in the air. People at the back begin to file out, shuffling as if they have all the time in the world.

Move, MOVE, I want to shout.

I should slap them hard across their arses with a stick to make them hurry, like you would aimless cattle. Rachel and Kate are as bad, waiting in turn for them all to lollop off from the row behind.

After you. No please, after you.

He hated it too, the odd time Mother could drag him here, all the standing about and polite chatter. 'Why should I be stuck in a cold church the one day I don't have to work? It's enough I've to listen to Marsham's orders all week, without him looking me over Sunday as well.' She did not answer, just looked at him funny.

Now at last they are moving and I take it back. Not cows, more like sheep with all their bleating and the way they mill about in the direction of the South Porch. What is wrong with walking in a straight line?

I drum my fingers on the pew as Mother sways onto the flagstones of the aisle. That queasy feeling in my stomach starts as I realise Thurtle has stopped nodding and smiling at Mrs Marsham and is coming over. No way to escape from the mustiness of this whitewashed place, out to where the hawthorn blossom is wafting through the air.

'Mrs Abrehart,' he says, wringing his hands in front of his long dress, which he calls a cassock, 'so good to see you this fine morning.'

'Reverend,' she responds, her voice its usual weary whisper.

He turns to my sisters. 'How are you two young ladies? I hope you're not giving your mother too much to worry about!'

They mumble their reply together. 'Good, good,' he blathers before focussing his piggy stare on me. 'Well, William. Many thanks for your fine efforts at the organ today – I felt quite out of breath watching your exertions.'

I ignore him, concentrating instead on my feet.

'Splendid. Must let you all be getting on – it's a glorious day outside. Let us hope some bright news comes through soon from the continent – right is on our side after all.'

More fidgeting of hands and muffled goodbyes, then Rachel takes Mother's arm and leads her towards the door. I edge out and start to follow the pair of them, but a cough and tap on the shoulder stops me.

'William, could I see you in the vestry about the arrangements for next week?' He marches between the pews, over to the curtain in the corner where he keeps his cloaks and things. I follow reluctantly.

'I thought you and I should have a little word.'

I stare at the floor. Black marble, faintly inscribed. Head down, do not look at his face.

Tobias Allington who Departed this Life November 12th, 1786. 43 Years.

Forty-three years, the same age he was.

'I can understand the depth of your sadness, William. A terrible business. But now is the time to put your grief aside. It would mean a lot to your mother.'

Mumble mumble mumble. I will not listen to his words.

'It must soon be coming up to the anniversary, mustn't it?'

No. One whole year and almost two weeks: he Departed this Life May 14th, 1939; today is May 26th 1940. Yesterday, a year ago, was the day they put him outside.

Into the ground.

'Look at me, William.' The Reverend places his hand on my shoulder, leaning in closer and staring at me to make my gaze meet his; the whites of his eyes are all yellow. 'Let us say a prayer together for your father. You can repeat my lines, if you like.'

'*Dear Lord*', he begins, the whole while fixing me with wonky face, willing me to join him. I stare down at the slab.

Let us remember John Abrehart,

The inside of my head starts to crackle. He is not yours to talk about!

Sorely missed by all who knew him,

Words hover at the tip of my tongue.

Particularly his beloved wife Louise, and children

The air is unmoving, cold like a tomb.

Rachel, Kate and William.

You are the head of the family now,

Lord, comfort them in their grief

Look after your mother and your sisters.

And keep him safe at your side

Shut your mouth. SHUT YOUR MOUTH

Until the day they are united once more

HE IS NOT COMING BACK.

In Your Eternal Paradise.

GO TO HELL. GO TO HELL YOU BLOODY OLD FOOL.

Amen.

My throat tingles in anticipation, but my lips remain tight. I want to punch his foolish face to stop him saying more. But I do not need to because he is shaking his head, his nose glowing like a big red beacon.

My silence has defeated him.

43

If he keeps on and on in future I will have to make sure he shuts his fat vicar mouth. He does not know anything! Not about what he is really like or the things we do together.

'It will truly be for the best when you desist from this, William – from this dumb show. Truly it will. It must cause your poor mother so much upset.'

He begins towards the altar then turns, almost as an after-thought: 'If you could help Mrs Thompson again at next week's matins it would be most appreciated.'

Outside, that interfering old cow Mrs Heckleton has collared Rachel – it is like she spends all of her time following us about. Mother stands beside his sticks while Kate pulls at the weeds growing tall off the spring sun and all the deadness below. Thurtle is wandering around, smiling at everyone and shaking hands like nothing has happened. I move beside Mother, but after a minute she starts off round the side of the church. I go to follow, but Kate grabs my sleeve.

'Leave her be, Billy. Here, help me get up this mess.'

And though I want to see that Mother is right, I do as my sister says and start tugging hard at all the held-fast thistles and dandelions, whose tangled roots go way, way down.

RACHEL

I know Tom's mother is avoiding me so I rush to catch her before she has time to scurry home. I don't want to call round later, because then I'll need an excuse for being there. She's trying to weave through the crowd in front of the archway, but they've slowed her progress and I'm catching up fast until I feel a bony hand on my forearm: Mrs Heckleton peering at me with her old-lady face, more lines than skin.

'How's your mother?'

I'm trapped, my target slipping away. I can't let her go – no news for so long now.

'She's over with Kate if you want a word.'

'Your brother was round here yesterday evening as I was seeing to Harold's stone. Gave me a right scare creeping about like that.'

Resigned, I force a smile, my head plotting how to contrive an accidental meeting later, when the Reverend gives me a reprieve. He snakes out of the crowd and calls over to Mrs Morley just as she is about to unhook the lychgate. She stops, and he has her.

'That your sister singing in the lane late last night?' Mrs Heckleton asks, a sly look on her face. I'm thinking how to answer when I notice the Reverend beginning to shuffle back this way.

'Must go – got to get started on dinner,' and I'm crunching across the stones, leaving her open-mouthed before she has a chance to make more of her little digs. I've timed it to perfection, the Reverend peeling off as I come alongside her.

'Mrs Morley!' I unlatch the gate and hold it open. 'Mind if I walk with you?' There's no point skirting around the subject, so I ask straight out before she can reply.

'Any word from Tom?'

She pauses, like she is gathering her thoughts, or at least her composure.

'Had a letter from him three weeks ago.'

'A letter?'

'Yes. It was quiet, he said, though I don't suppose it's that way any longer – must be getting bad over there for the King to declare today a day of prayer.'

45

'The wireless was on at the Hall yesterday. The Colonel reckons it won't be long before Mr Churchill brings them all back over here to defend our own shores rather than waste a load of effort on the French and Belgians.'

'Well, let's hope so.'

I nod and we walk on in silence. I glance across at her face. She is the same age as Mother, but you wouldn't guess because she looks so much younger. She's tiny – petite is the word, I think – with thick reddish hair and skin that shines; she's different now to before though, more tired-looking since Tom left.

'I'm worried for him, Rachel. Don't want him to come back like my husband did.'

Mr Morley lost half of one of his legs in the first war. He died much later – I'm not sure what of, some sort of accident, I think – when I was small; just Tom and her after that. I remember him a little, he didn't seem to want to talk to people much – not even us children – like no longer being whole was an embarrassment. I asked Tom once if he'd seen the skin where the leg had come off. All smooth, he said, with a pink crease down the middle. Father didn't think much of Mr Morley. One time he even made Tom cry when we were playing in the garden; he didn't realise Tom was there and stood laughing with another man from the farm about Peg Leg's withered little stump. In contrast, he had only one small wound from the war – his French souvenir he called it – a two-inch gash in his shin made by a sliver of shrapnel. One evening in the bath he pulled a whole ear of corn out of it. It was sprouting and he planted it next day in the garden. Miracle wheat he said, though I don't think it ever did end up growing.

'He'll be fine, I'm sure of it,' I say, my heart racing as I picture Tom in the midst of all those bombs and guns. We're passing the wall that hides the Marshams' house, past where the yellowing ivy-flowers will summon swarms of noisy bees in a few months' time. Nothing now though, only our footsteps on the road. A breeze is beginning to build, like that early spring evening with Tom, two years ago.

We walked, our fingers interlocked, along the darkness of the lane, cutting across the churchyard, where he pressed his foot on the bottom string of wire and yanked up the twisted tangle above. I slid between, before doing the same for him. Once

46

through, I knew where to head for: straight for the far side, the corner where the silence shrouds the trees. But he held me back, taking my hand again in his before dropping something cold into my palm. The clouds were thick, gauzing the moon, but the breeze was strong and soon there was a break and I could see it glisten in the whiteness: a bracelet made of tiny golden links.

'It's beautiful.'

I held Tom's hand tight and he led me across the black meadow to our special place. Inside we laid down a blanket and lit the candles we'd stowed before in a gap beneath the floorboards: the soft shadows they threw on the walls made the house feel almost like a home again after all those abandoned years fending for itself.

'When William was little I told him there were ghosts here.'

'Ghosts? Ever seen any?'

'No. You don't see them – you can only hear them. Listen.'

Silent as statues we lay, the cold marble of his bare skin pressing against me. His dark eyes were fixed on mine, unblinking. The sole sound was the wind waking the branches outside.

'Can't hear nothing,' he said.

'Wait.'

'But I want you too much,' and he stroked his middle finger against my bellybutton, running it down before it came to my other hairs and he began twirling them.

'Stop!' I giggled.

'What do you want me to do then?' And I was gazing at him, then murmuring, as he put the finger into his mouth and drew it out, glistening, before bringing it lower. He slipped it inside me, joining our bodies as one beneath the hesitant glow of the candles.

'Do you want to come in?' Mrs Morley is saying, and I have to catch myself as we arrive at her cottage.

'I should get going,' I say, desperate now for space alone with my thoughts.

'Can show you the letter, if you like.'

I follow into the darkness of her kitchen, which is illuminated when she flicks the switch by the door. She had the electricity put in after her husband died, the first house in the village apart from the Marshams'. I wait by the table, which is round and covered with a red checkerboard cloth, as she lights the stove and stands the kettle on top.

'Have a seat. I'll go find it.'

On the windowsill are two photographs: one of her and Tom when he was a little boy; and another, more recent, of him in his army get-up. He stares at the camera all stern and proper, but his cap is a little skew-whiff which makes him look less serious. His face is blurred and indistinct – he must have moved slightly just as the picture was taken – which makes him seem even further from me. I have never seen him dressed that army way in the flesh, only in my dream. It came again last night; each time it is identical:

William rushes into the garden where I am hanging the washing, clamouring that Tom has come home. I race to his house and it's true – he's standing out front, so handsome in his uniform. As I approach it takes all my strength not to dissolve under the gaze of those deep-pooled eyes. But as my fingers reach for the familiarity of his face, something changes. Tom has vanished from the empty lane and, roughly awakened, I lie gasping for air in the gloom.

Mrs Morley comes back in, stirring me from my thoughts, and fetches two cups from the pantry; she puts them down on the table, alongside the letter. My heart races at the sight of his handwriting. I scan the black ink, but can't concentrate on the clumsy lines – schoolwork wasn't ever his strongpoint – because I'm too busy thinking: why have you never once written to me?

Then near the bottom, I pick out my name and my eyes focus in. *How is Rachel?*

My hands quiver like Mother's as I try and hold the sheet steady. I fold it in half and pass it back.

'It's a nice letter,' I say, though inside I am longing for more – more than just words on a page.

'Yes,' she says, 'his writing's still rotten though,' and we both laugh. She's smiling now and it seems her guard has dropped; I can't keep my feelings inside any longer.

'Why'd he have to leave that way? We had it worked out. We were going to get married and everything, but then he just went off.'

She shrugs, but an oddness about her expression makes me think she's hiding something. And then it comes to me.

48

'Did my father say anything?'

She is quiet, like she is weighing up what to say. The kettle explodes in a whistle of steam and she gets up to pour, swishing a little of the water around to warm the blue-and-white pot.

'I'm not sure,' she says, almost in a whisper.

'He did, didn't he?'

A pained frown comes across her face before she answers. 'I don't know, Rachel. You'd have to ask him.'

'Can't though, can I?'

'No.'

'Well now *he's* gone, Tom can come home and it can all be like it used to be.'

'I don't think it's as simple as that.'

'Why? I don't mind.'

'Oh Rachel...'

'I had a feeling he'd said something because why else would Tom go off without a word? Not with how it was between us. I'm not stupid.'

'Perhaps your father wanted to protect you, Rachel.'

'So he did!'

She looks down at the floor and I am fuming because now I am sure who is responsible – only he is in the earth so there is nothing I can do to get back at him, except I should go straight to the churchyard and dance on top of his grave.

'But why didn't *you* keep Tom from leaving, Mrs Morley?'

She goes over to the sink and I stare at the tablecloth until my eyes no longer focus and the red squares merge so that I am in that empty shell of a house again. Only, as Tom and I lie listening for the people from way back, the scene in my head is a new one:

We are still both naked, and his goose-pimpled skin still cold against mine. This time though, instead of doing those things he's so good at, he sits suddenly up, his spine rigid.

'What?' I say.

'You hear that?'

'No. Nothing.'

'There!' and now I do catch something half-lost in the night: all these different voices clamouring together and then a child whispering incessantly above them:

'Him. It is him.'

49

I get up too and pull one of the blankets around myself; the voices are nearer and Tom is trying to peer through the windows, only he can't see anything so is running frantically from one side of the room to the other. The noise has become deafening and now the child is crying out, a terrible sound which makes me jerk back with a start onto the tiles of Mrs Morley's kitchen, where she crouches, cradling my head and holding a vial under my nose.

'It's alright, Rachel. You fainted for a minute. You're fine now.'

But I'm not fine. I'm sitting on the floor with my arms flopped around the mother of the man I love but cannot have, and I need to get away because my father has spoiled everything. I cannot bear Tom's blurred army-face gawking at me from his photograph and have to look away through the window into the blankness of the sky, breathing in deep and slow to keep myself from going off again.

'I should get home. Start dinner.'

'Don't be silly. You can't when you've just fainted.'

But I'm up and out of the door, passing unsteadily alongside the farm's wall and its coiled ivy before she can stop me, ignoring her shouts to wait. I race past the empty churchyard, past William chopping logs in the garden, into the kitchen where Mother sits like nothing at all has changed.

Even though everything has.

Now I am certain: Tom's feelings for me are just as strong as before, and I do not care why he went off that way, because it was not what he wanted, just what *he* made him do. My father – who has spoiled everything with his selfishness, who has put Tom in the middle of such terrible dangers just because he could not bear the thought of what people might say.

I turn and shout at Mother: 'Did you know too?' Though of course she's not listening, so what is the point?

Only now, there's a point to all of it.

WILLIAM

The blade of the chopper smashes against the grain of the wood with a dull thwock, as I imagine bringing it down, hard, across the back of the Reverend's neck.

There is already plenty of firewood piled under the lean-to beside the privy. One time, I got a good clip round the lughole from him after I chalked *Shit House* on its black door; I knew I would get wrong, but once the idea came I could not stop. He was laughing later, though, when he helped me scrub the words before Mother noticed.

Still time before dinner. The three of them are inside getting it ready. Faint blossom-perfume wafts past my nose as the apple tree creaks in the breeze. He could always be found here on Sundays, splitting logs into chunks for the kitchen grate. I try to copy the smoothness of his action, and soon the swing of my arms and the sway of the branches sends me thinking about him again. About his last autumn.

The wind has been blowing a gale all week, rattling the flimsy pane of my window and wheezing through the jagged slit against the frame so at night I have to burrow under the blankets to escape its chill reach. It does not die away until long after dinner, then him and me go out to collect storm-blown wood. The pair of us work through the spinney at the side of the road to Summer End, gathering up armfuls of the smaller stuff and piling it in the ditch so he can come with a cart when he finishes at the farm the next day to bring it home. Lichen off the branches I am carrying powders the front of my jacket.

'Winter's almost on us,' he says, 'Everything in here will soon be dead.'

'What happens to us when we die?' I ask, and when he has slung across another log he leans against the trunk of a tall sweet chestnut to get back his breath.

'You go to church. Don't you listen to what the Reverend has to say about it?'

'Yes. He says our souls rise to heaven.'

I think about the dead things I have seen: stiff-legged calves on their sides in the meadow, bloating and buzzing with bluebottles in the summer heat; shrivelled sucked-out birds half the size they should be; and the stray cat Joe Scott and I found in a keeper's trap over where they rear the pheasants, its tongue hanging down all swollen and wrong. What happened to their souls? I can see how a bird's could flutter from its tiny parched body, but how would a cat or cow's know where it was going?

'Do animals go too?'

He shrugs. 'Some don't believe there's even a heaven for people.'

'The Reverend says they're sinners.'

'Or they might be right and him wrong.' He grins at me.

I have never thought of this before but now it makes sense, because the Reverend's nose is plum-red and puffed up and when he stands close to you his breath stinks.

'Do you know what happens?'

He shrugs. 'I reckon when it comes we lie under the earth, becoming less and less, till one day not even a single fingernail remains. The only things we leave behind are our children, and the thoughts people have about us. Once they're gone that's it. Should think it's like falling asleep and never waking up.'

I stand quiet for a minute trying to take this all in, because it is different to the things the Reverend says in church and Miss Hexham teaches us at school.

'So has Grandfather Sampson completely gone now?

'No. Because your mother is his daughter, and a part of him. And I still remember him, as do lots of others.'

'I was only a baby when the horse kicked him,' I say. 'What about Grandfather Abrehart?'

'Gone the same way.'

'Did a horse get him too?'

'No. He died when I was a boy. That's why we moved.'

His face looks sad and he starts hauling a big piece of elm across the floor – it hisses like a grass snake as it drags a trail through the leaves.

'Is his soul in Heaven?'

'Listen. I'll tell you something,' he says, turning round and staring at me with a funny grin, 'though I may be wrong. When I was in the trenches I didn't see a single soul rise up out of all

52

those bodies lying there in the mud. Some of the others reckoned on visions of angels and spirits, but I only saw the dead and the dying. Hundreds of them.'

I am confused and his words are scuttling around my head, twisting into thousands and thousands of pale, floating shapes – blue and see-through like the lantern man's light – disappearing into the darkness until they become distant wisps of clouds.

'We're skin, bone and memories, that's all. So it's up to you to remember me when I go, alright William? Don't ever forget, or that'll be it. One day your son will do the same for you.' He smiles and ruffles my hair and I drop another armful of logs onto the stockpile, not sure what to make of it all.

'Look. A storm-cock,' he says, motioning to the top of the chestnut; I see it perched way up, all brown and speckled. 'They like to make a racket after a big blow.' He has stopped now and stares all serious at me. 'Enjoy yourself while you've got the chance, William. It's harder when you're older. Too many temptations and disappointments.'

I sling across a final dead snag, a cluster of tiny holes bored through its bark into the heartwood beneath. The storm-cock begins to whistle his tune as the last of the leaves drift down:

'To whom shall I tell my sorrow?' he sings. 'To whom shall I tell my sorrow?'

The blade jars through a knot in the log, wedging into the stump below, shavings of wood splintering past my face. The wood, which has a greenness about it, comes from an old ash which, with the elm, is the commonest tree round here. It will burn even and steady: not like the spitting logs of pine or sweet chestnut that shower their sparks onto the hearthrug. One time a cinder flew right across the room and landed on the square of matting where we wipe our boots by the door, sending it alight so that he had to hurry like a madman and stamp it to black.

I chop with precision, making sure the pieces are just right. Doing this will at least keep Rachel from crazing me the rest of the day and I can wander the woods while the sun is still worth something. I chop faster and faster because thinking of him has made my eyes moisten and I do not want to let my sisters catch me bawling like a baby – they would not understand because it was not the same between them as between me and him.

To whom shall I tell my sorrow?

There is no one – nothing – since he went, which is why I am this way. Nothing but the birds and the trees.

Will it make things any better if I tell it all to them?

RACHEL

A spray of water stings my arm as I drop the potatoes into the boiling foam; in any case, the pain is fleeting and doesn't matter: I feel stronger, more calm, now I know: he has not forgotten me.

Kate perches sallow-faced at the table. Mother is upstairs in her room, asleep or dreaming as usual. William's frantic chopping still sounds from the side of the house – I pray he won't have his fingers off because he gets so involved I wonder if he concentrates properly on the job in hand. I lift the lid on the other pot, churning the stew with a spoon. Its smell welcomes me in, as I only had one piece of toast for breakfast and sitting through the Reverend's riddle of a sermon gives you a long time to think about how hungry you are. Why can't he just say a simple prayer to let them all come home safe?

'You have to?' Kate asks. She sits at the table looking poorly.

'Have to what?'

'Keep stirring it over my way. Making me sniff it. You know I don't feel right.'

'Whose fault's that?'

'At least I know how to have fun.'

I turn away and concentrate on the cutting, digging out a black eye buried deep in the potato's off-white flesh. Thinking back to the dance, I wonder if perhaps she's right, if I am no longer capable of enjoying myself. Not like her. I'm envious of her naivety for a second, until I remember how she let herself get.

'You sat there so miserable all night,' she says. 'Would've scared any men right off.'

'Least I didn't make a complete fool of myself.'

'You liar, Rachel.'

I say nothing.

'I didn't, did I? Was I that bad?'

'You were singing on the way home. Mrs Heckleton heard you.'

'But I only had a couple of drinks. Will he hate me?' She goes silent for a minute, then smirks. 'He's lovely though, isn't he?'

'His hair's quite nice, I suppose.'

He reminds me a little of Tom. His clothes, I think, even though the uniform is a different colour, because really he's not

55

anything like Tom to look at. He was talking loud, his mouth close to my ear, and I could hardly understand him above the noise of the music and people circling round the hall. I nodded every so often and, when I glanced across, his gooseberry-green eyes were staring into mine. He's tall with strong, thick arms yet his hair is boyish and fair, his fringe flopping over his forehead. I can see why Kate thinks she is in love with him – all that easy charm and big London talk. Not like Tom: always quiet, never letting his mouth spoil the moment; the intensity of his stare bewitching me every time.

'Isn't it? And he's so tall and strong. I really do like him, Rachel.'

After I came back from outside they were away among the crowd, so I sat apart, shut off by the music, not wanting to talk to or dance with anyone; I haven't the desire to pretend any more. All them others must have sensed it because no one asked me, though one or two from the base came as if they were going to speak before thinking better of it. When I looked across the dance floor again the two of them were nowhere and I wondered about going to find her in case she was in trouble, but then David was leading her through the doorway, and then bringing us drinks, which Kate knocked back like water.

'Did he say anything about me?'

'You were the one draped over him all night.'

She giggles. 'We didn't have much time for talking! But he was chatting to you for an age when we came inside – he must've said something.'

'Just about what the other men in his crew – the pilot and whatnot – are like; how he worries whether they'll make it back in one piece each time they go out.'

'Didn't he mention me at all?'

'He thought you were looking very pretty.'

'He did?'

'Said he doesn't usually go in for blonde girls – he prefers darker hair – but he thinks you're sweet.'

'Go on.'

'I don't know. He was asking about the rest of us. Is it only us two? What do our parents do...'

If Kate didn't manage to scare him off last night I wonder what he'll make of us if he ever does come round? In one way it's good he wants to find out more because that means he's serious about her, though I hate to imagine how we'll appear. Shame he didn't see us before when things were normal, it wouldn't have been so awkward. Though I suppose then there would have been Father around to spoil things for her too.

'What did you say?'

What does she think I told him? That our father's dead, our little brother's given up speaking, and our mother's given up living?

'Not a lot. Just that it's me, you, William and Mother. He asked how old you are, too.'

'Oh.' Her eager expression changes. 'You didn't, did you?'

'Didn't what? Tell him? Course I did. What was I meant to say?'

'Why'd you go and do that? I'd already told him I was eighteen. You always have to stuff things up for me!'

'Well I didn't know,' I laugh, not quite sure why she's acting so upset. 'Worse things I could have said! That'll teach you to go lying to people about your age.'

'Oh that's right. You're so lily-white.'

'You can't invent things like that. He was always going to find out.'

'But it's only a few months. Doesn't make any difference.'

'Fine. So why'd you say it?'

'Because you've never lied about anything, have you? You think you're so clever!'

But I'm not; I know I'm the biggest fool going. Because I let Tom slip away when I should have stopped him. Or even better, gone off with him when he left. Then the other would have turned out right and the bad would not have happened.

'What about when you lied to Mother and Father about the ice?'

'The ice! Not that again. That was years ago, Kate. Can't believe you even remember. Anyway, I didn't lie. Just didn't say. It's different.'

I remember though, the winter the water froze solid for weeks. I took her and William – she would have been about seven, he was just a toddler – to the pit behind the farm. Don't know why but this compulsion came over me and, even though I knew it was wrong, I had to do it. At that moment I didn't care about consequences because the thought was already too much in my head. I took William's hand and we started sliding across the ice; Kate kept slipping over and got scared so soon ran back, but he was having a great laugh, jumping up and down as we went further out. When we got to the middle we stopped, and everything was so peaceful and quiet with the snow in the fields deadening all the noise, like the whole world had come to a standstill. Then I felt it crack, so started dragging him furiously to the other side, panic growing in my stomach that any moment we would disappear straight through. The pond seemed like a vast lake, the land a world away; Kate was screaming and William virtually flying as I pulled him along. When we staggered onto the far bank a wave of relief came over me and I hugged William so hard he cried. Kate said she'd tell, but I made her promise on her life she'd keep it a secret.

Tell-tale tit. Your tongue shall be split.

I never act that way now. Never do anything against the grain, just stay on the sidelines and wait for whatever's going to happen to happen. Perhaps I should be more reckless, like Kate, and start chasing the things I want. Only now, those things have gone and I can't get them back just by running at the empty air.

She pipes up again. No stopping her once her teeth are bared.

'How about when you started carrying on with Tom? You told some tales to keep that quiet!'

I stop mixing around the contents of the pot and look across. Her eyes are big and sparkling – I can tell she's furious and wants to make me upset. And it's working, because my cheeks are prickling and getting hot, but I won't let her see that she's won. She doesn't understand the real world and the things that happen to real people. To her it's all dancing and sweethearts.

'Stop it, Kate. You don't know nothing.'

'I know plenty,' she says, determined to get me riled.

'No you don't. You've no business to talk about what me and Tom have.'

'Had. If you've noticed, he's not here with you any more. Ran off to the army, if you remember! Preferred to get shot at than stay here with you.'

'Be quiet!' My eyes are starting to moisten; I can tell she's enjoying seeing me this way.

'He's not coming back, Rachel. Probably got another girl by now. I think I overheard Mrs Heckleton mention it.'

This can't be true – she's saying it because she wants to needle me. Mrs Morley would've told me and his letter wouldn't have asked: *How is Rachel?* Would it? Unless perhaps he really has met someone and that's why he wanted to find out how I am, before breaking the news.

'Liar!' I spit out the word. 'At least I know who Tom is. Shouldn't think you can even tell me your precious David's surname? Though now he realises you're only a girl I suppose he'll be off.'

She stands there all hardened, wearing an odd look as if she's about to reply with something that will strike me dumb. I want to wipe the stupid expression straight off her face. Her bottom lip drops and I wonder what's going to fall out, but then the malice in her eyes fades and she focuses on the floor.

'You've no idea,' she mutters, and I snort, not even bothering to respond to her nonsense. She's still pulling that face and I glare back at her. She can say what she likes, it doesn't matter because she will never experience anything with her airman – or anyone else – as pure as the bond between Tom and me. And it will be like that again soon, only stronger, when he comes back. Because reading my name in his letter makes me certain he feels the same way too. What she said about him finding somebody new is nonsense. She's the one with no idea.

I turn around; at some point Mother has wisped into the kitchen, silent as usual. Outside, the thack-thack of William's axe echoes louder than ever. Kate gets up from the table and stands beside me: a half-hearted gesture of reconciliation? William's rhythm grows faster, pounding into me and mixing with the meaty stench of dinner. My head's swirling, even though I drank hardly anything at the dance. I look across at my sister – she's ignoring me, and I have to say one last thing because I hate the way she's so sure of herself.

'Well don't come to me when David makes a fool of you.'

'Don't worry, you'll be the last person,' she replies, staring at me with those cold blue eyes.

Now I feel guilty for goading her and want to explain. Only I can't think what to say, except that when she was talking all

59

that foolishness last night perhaps she was right: she better had start running from this place, else before long she really might turn to stone.

Just like the rest of us.

WILLIAM

Brown stew steams on the plate before me, all we ever seem to eat. I am starving and could do with a good feed – chopping has given me a right appetite. It is lucky I am so handy at catching rabbits, because we would turn to nothing if we only had the meat we get on ration. When he gutted them I never did like the rawness. Now I am used to it, though I do not look too hard at all the blood and try to forget it was ever a living animal running and burrowing through the fields. That way the mess is worth putting up with, as the meat tastes delicious. The most important thing he showed me is as soon as the rabbit is dead you have to start squeezing, else when you take out all the insides the bladder will burst and spoil everything. You hold it in one hand – its legs hanging down all limp – and press hard with the other on its stomach so the piss squirts onto the ground. Then you can go in with a knife.

'I'm not hungry. Don't want none,' Kate says, pushing her plate away.

'Maybe you had something made you bad at Audrey's.'

Rachel is staring at her, grinning slightly, but Kate's face is like stone. Her eyes are hollow and moisture glistens on her forehead. I am looking at her too, because I am sure they are lying about last night. Mother will not realise with the way she is, but they must take me for an idiot. She is whispering away, mouthing grace I think, though so quiet I can hardly hear, let alone anyone up in Heaven. I do not know why she bothers – he never once felt the need to say it.

Besides, if Kate and Rachel were at Audrey and Rose's why did they come back after midnight with an air man wearing a uniform? They are wrong and I am onto them – I was watching when they came across the grass. They are not going to trick me because I promised, and if they get into trouble again it will all be my fault – I can guess what will happen if I let them go about with soldiers and air men, because of before.

So I know my sisters are not telling the truth.

61

Rachel and Mother are at the table waiting when he comes in from mending a fence over the back of the meadow. It is July and the light will hold up for a while, so I am looking forward to going about after tea. I am in the corner reading a book about trees that I have borrowed from school. He is whistling like he sometimes does and, when he has taken off his boots and jacket, goes across to the table.

'What we having?' he asks. But he answers his own question before she can reply when he sees the leftover stew on the plates, along with carrots, potatoes and runner beans. 'Coney again, is it?' he says, and sits down.

Now I take my seat opposite Mother, and Kate comes next to me; he is on the end, as ever: the head of the family.

'Get stuck in!' and he has barely picked up his cutlery when Rachel says, 'There's...' She stops because he already has meat and potato skewered on his fork and is putting it into his mouth.

'What?' he replies, though it sounds more like a grunt with all the food in the way. She does not continue, but instead Mother speaks:

'John – Rachel has some news.'

He sets his knife and fork down on the plate, though he is still chewing like a cow, his mouth grinding round and round.

'Go on.'

He carries on bolting it down and so do I, but all the while Rachel's fork hovers above her food as she looks across at Mother. Then, after the longest pause, my sister speaks and the room goes funeral quiet.

'I'm expecting.'

Outside the swifts screech like devils as their blackness streaks past the window, whirling up to the eaves above my bedroom where they build their flimsy nests.

'Expecting what?' he replies, his face curving into a big smile as he winks at me. Then silence again and he is staring straight at her, but not saying anything at all.

'How long you known about this?' he asks Mother.

'A day or two.'

He does not look at Rachel but over to me, still grinning, 'That's a turn up, eh William?' I am not sure what to say so nod my head.

62

'Well, what's done is done. These things happen.' He picks his knife and fork back up and starts shovelling down the rest of his food; I follow his lead.

'Don't let it get cold!'

Rachel, Kate and Mother start too – though they are picking at it rather than properly tucking in – and the only noise apart from the swifts outside is the chink of cutlery on china. After a bit, he fills the room's wordlessness.

'Whose is it then?' His eyes fix straight at Rachel, but she looks down, saying nothing. 'Don't tell me you don't know?' he says, like it is a big joke. And he nudges me with his elbow, but I am not sure what is happening so concentrate on cutting away the fat from my meat.

'Come on! Who?' and his voice is a little louder now, before Mother pipes up, sounding almost angry.

'Leave her be, John, she doesn't want to say.'

'Well we're going to have to find out sooner or later, so why not now?' He prods a finger into his mouth and flicks a lump of gristle onto the side of his plate.

'I don't want to,' Rachel mumbles. I am trying not to meet his gaze and can see Kate is too, both of us bowing our heads like we are in church.

'Who did it to you?' He gets up from the table and starts pacing about the room.

She does not answer.

'Come on, Rachel. I need to know. Who?' He has stopped moving and is standing next to me, his palms pressed into the oak as he glares across at her. She whispers in a voice I cannot properly hear, and neither can he. 'Speak up!'

Again. Only this time I can make it out and so can everyone else.

'A soldier from the base.'

'Really! This man have a name?'

'I don't know.'

'Well that's handy – the unknown bloody soldier! Surprised it wasn't the Archangel Gabriel, don't you reckon William?'

I say nothing, because I am still not exactly certain what is happening, so just keep prodding my fork at the grey rabbit meat.

'Sure it wasn't someone from round here? Someone we know?' He has calmed, but I can tell he is angry like I have never seen before, because something is changed about the way his eyes look.

She shakes her head and he slams his fist on the table, which bows in the middle.

'Tell me!' he shouts, and the plates jump into the air, bits of food spilling over their sides and the china moving a little closer to the edge with each blow, until one comes smashing to the floor. Blue-and-white shards poke from the sludge of stew below, along with lumps of orange, green and pale – the carrots, beans and potatoes.

Rachel has started to sob and so has Kate. I rise from my chair and try to make myself small in the corner, out of the way. I pick up my book and try and read the words – 'The ash (*Fraxinus excelsior)* can grow to heights of over one hundred feet' – but all the time I am really looking over at him. He stops banging the table and walks round behind Rachel. He pulls her up by her hair and shouts into her mouth:

'WHY COULD YOU NOT KEEP YOUR LEGS TOGETHER?' He lets go and she is on the floor, her elbows wrapped in front of her chest, rocking from side-to-side and whimpering.

'YOU LITTLE WHORE!' And as he says it he is like a slathering dog, spittle flying from his mouth as the words fire out. She covers her face with her shuddering hands, but I can see the tiny bubbles of his fury glinting on her fingers in the low-angled sunlight that has crept into the room.

He walks to the door, slamming it open so that it rattles the wall. I watch through the window as his silhouette disappears up the drove, black against the bleeding sky.

Kate is hugging Rachel, the pair of them wailing together on the floor. Mother has remained at the table, her mouth stretched and tight like she is smiling, her face all wet.

Only, she is not smiling.

I go over and she pulls me onto her knee, holding my head tight to her chest so I can hardly breathe, but I do not care. He does not return that night and for hours we do not move from where we are: fortunately the evening is warm, because the door stays wide for an age before I dare close it.

I am scared when I get home from school next day in case I should find something terrible. But inside is unchanged, except

64

the pieces of broken plate and food have gone from the floor. Mother and Rachel and Kate are sitting like nothing has happened, though they are too upright for it to be any old day. I prop myself next to them, hoping that the real him – the one who takes me round the woods and shows me secret things, and who never gets angry – will return.

'How's your day been, William?' he asks when he comes in and I wonder if it is all a trick and he is going to repeat his rage. He sits down to tea in silence, like last evening did not happen. When we are eating the pudding, which is stewed apples and custard, he turns to Rachel:

'I'm sorry. I'll not be that way again.'

She does not reply.

'We'll help you take care of it, won't we, Mother?' and for once she is listening and nodding. 'But you won't have nothing more to do with that one, do you hear? Don't go thinking I'm a fool.'

Rachel's head is slumped so she does not have to hold his gaze, and as she whispers 'yes' I can see her eyes welling.

He kept his promise because he did not lose his temper again, and made sure Rachel was looked after right: the baby too, who was not my sister but my niece. She was called Laura and was so small and sickly when she popped out that Doctor Howell thought she might not even make it through the first few days. But she did. Afterwards, Mother and him made out like she was my little sister so that people would not think wrong of Rachel, but I am not sure that anyone in the village was really tricked.

When she was hardly bigger than my hands put together, Rachel let me hold her on my knee. She wriggled and I had to cradle the back of her head because when they are like that there are no muscles in their necks, so they can snap clean off if you are not careful.

Her skin was pink and soft as velvet; only later did it change colour.

It happened when we were about to eat, all except Laura who was upstairs in her cot. She was still too young to have proper food, instead suckling on Rachel like a kitten snuggled up to a mother cat. He said he would go check on her before he sat down – because she was grizzling and grumbling – and that we should start without him and not wait. We are all chattering and eating and after a few minutes I have forgotten about Laura's noises and him being away. When he appears in the doorway I do not see him for a second because he is so quiet and still, staring empty-eyed into the room and not looking at anybody in particular. Mother notices him too.

'What's the matter, John?' she asks.

But he does not reply, keeps looking over the tops of all our heads. Then Rachel rises, wearing a worried look, and her and mother and Kate move urgently out the room and up the stairs and after a minute there is a wail of noise and in the racket I can make out Rachel shouting.

'SHE IS BLUE, SHE IS BLUE.'

He blunders over to the table and collapses into his chair, still not saying nothing, and now Kate is back down ordering me to run and use the telephone at the farm to ring for help. I get up the road in record quick time and Mrs Marsham's face whitens when I tell her, bringing me inside while she dials the number, even though I still have on my boots, which shed their mud on the carpet. But by the time Doctor Howell arrives from Summer End there is nothing he can do to save Rachel's baby, who is not my sister but my niece.

'This happens sometimes when they arrive early and are delicate like her,' the Doctor says afterwards. 'They stop breathing in their sleep, or have something wrong inside them that we didn't know was there.'

Later on a police man came from Lynn to examine the cot and ask us all questions about Laura, because he needed to report to the corner man whether anything was amiss, though he was sorry, he said, to have to pry at this sad time. He was the same one came round after I found him, asking me all sorts of things until Doctor Howell took him outside and talked with him, his hands flapping up and down excitedly as they stood by the hedge.

If I were bigger, I told them. If only I were bigger.

We were all very sad, except Rachel who put on a stone face; but he was the worst, because he loved his granddaughter too much and he was there when it happened and could do nothing to save her. I could not stand to see him silent-crying all the while, which I had never known him do before, punching one fist into the open palm of the other and muttering away to himself. But most of all I could not bear to be inside the house because it did not seem like a proper home once Laura's noises no longer filled it, even though before they crazed me when they made me come awake in the black of the night.

So I must look after my sisters, because I do not want Rachel to be so sad again – or even Kate – because then they might end up where he and Laura are now, and I must not let that happen. They must never become the words he called her as he stood raging – Joe Scott told me later what they meant – and be opening up their legs for any soldiers or air men.

Because, although I did not like to see him so angry, he was right: having babies is too sad.

And perhaps he knew, even then, how it would all turn out.

MOTHER

Rachel and William sit opposite, cutting me adrift from the world; Kate is to my right, closest to the fire and the embers burning black at the bottom of the grate. Even among the room's shadows my youngest daughter looks fragile, her food abandoned and unfinished. Am I too late to say grace? Father always took delight in speaking those words, even though he was never a religious man.

'We are grateful for the nourishment on our plates and the company of family...'

And Albert Sampson is tucking in beside them once more, the pleasure across his face plain to see, smiling and talking as he chews, mopping spilled gravy from the sides of his mouth with a crust of bread, asking Louise, Mother and Nan if anything of note has happened, before telling of the day's events at the Estate: about the grey horse gone lame; the swallows nesting beneath a plough in a barn; or how the Colonel dropped by for a few minutes in his fancy car, a ramshackle parade-ground of farmhands doffing their caps as he passed.

Now Father, Nan and Mother are gone, replaced at the table by John and the two little girls, rinsed in the same shadow-light. William is still growing inside the fit-to-burst oval of Louise's belly.

'Kicking again, John. You want to feel?'

He stretches his arm across and places it on her. The baby thumps twice.

'Got a strong boot on him. What makes you so sure it's a boy?'

'Seems different. To how the others were, I mean.'

'What do you think about that, girls? Would you like a little brother?' They both are smirking and nodding.

'Can we dress him up like Dolly and take him for walks, Daddy?' Kate replies. She is four-and-a-half, her hair curly and golden.

'Well, I don't know about that!'

'You're silly, Kate,' says Rachel, who even though she was born only two years before her sister, already has something

about her – perhaps her dark eyes, or the way her black hair falls like a plumb-line against the side of her face – that makes her seem much older.

'*He won't want to be a dolly. He'll want to be a soldier, like Daddy. Can we dress him up as a soldier, Mummy, can we?*'

Louise is about to answer but is transfixed by a sudden image of John – the yellowing photograph he showed her not long after they met, as they crouched inside the shell of the place in which he was born. She is cross-legged on the floorboards, her stomach fluttering as he leans across holding out the tattered paper.

'*That's me. In the middle. Those other two were my pals from training.*'

In the photograph three young men in uniform are posing on a short flight of steps leading up to a church doorway. A crease obscures part of the man on the right. He is not looking at the camera but away at something in the opposite top corner, his arms behind his back. The left-hand man has a black moustache and an ammunition belt that hangs diagonally across his shoulder; he is smoking a cigarette. John stands between them, giving a quizzical expression to the lens. With his hair hidden by his cap and the collar of his jacket clasped tight about his neck it is hard to tell how different his time-frozen features appear to those of the man beside her now.

'*Somewhere in Kent. We were off not long after. The other two – Ernest and Albert...*' *He stops, the pitch of his voice rising.* '*Can't even remember their surnames – they got it almost as soon as it started.*'

'*You poor thing,*' *she replies, reaching out to his face.*

'*It's alright,*' *John says, as she wipes away the wet.* '*I'm one of the lucky ones. Pure-bottled luck – like your father says.*'

She knows, at this moment, that she must comfort him, so brings her other hand around to the back of his head, pulling him towards her. But he does not respond, instead sobbing in breathless coughs that rake through his entire body.

'*Poor thing,*' *she repeats, smearing her thumb across his cheek. This close, she notices, his eyes are not black but the darkest of browns. The whites – usually so bright and clear – are threaded with tiny red lines.*

'It'll be better now. You're here with us. With me.' She caresses his head as he rocks back and forth, his knees tucked hard to his chest, while in another time and place the six-year old Rachel asks:

'Please can we dress the baby as a soldier, Mummy?'

And the yet-to-be-born William is kicking inside her again, and her daughters are begging until she cannot bear to listen to their tiny voices any longer.

'No! No boy of mine will wear a uniform!'

John is telling Rachel that everything is all right, that Mother is tired and didn't mean it, but in any case Rachel does not look upset, just confused. Unlike Kate, whose frightened eyes dart from John to Louise as her mother cries out:

'He won't have to, will he, John?'

And the three of them are staring at me, like they are in the moment too – William's fork paused in front of his mouth – before Rachel speaks.

'Mother, are you alright?'

Am I? Even though there is nothing left in the now, because it is all trapped in the way-back along with everything else that was good? And, if I lift my head for even a moment, to try to forget, I am somewhere else, then somewhere else and then...

The end of the drove stirs.

Haze and road merge, revealing a distant figure on a bicycle, tottering beside the mound of grass growing wild down the track's centre. The hedge is white, a replica of the first time he came this way. Only now, not hoar frost but clusters of pale Mayblossom floating in circles, like a snowstorm whipped high by the gathering gusts.

'He's coming.' And this time I will change things – this time it will be different.

'Who is?' says Kate, stroking me gently on the hand.

'John.'

There is a silence around the table, not even broken by the birds warbling outside.

'He's gone, Mother. You know that, don't you?'

'He's coming again. Down the drove. Look.'

William is on his feet and at the window; his sisters rise too, and now the three of them are peering in rapt concentration. My

70

mouth forms a smile as I wait. William looks intent, staring across like a cat about to ambush its prey, his pupils big and excited.

'It's him. Rachel, it's him!' Kate is shouting. 'I knew he'd come!' She grabs William's hands and twirls him in a little waltz by the fireplace, but he pulls away and returns to the window. Now as he turns around and looks at me his eyes are smaller, scrunched-up.

'Will I do?' Kate asks Rachel, brushing down her dress. 'Haven't time to change!'

He reaches the bottom of the garden and is getting off the bicycle, leaning it against the hedge – carefully this time, not falling like before; Kate's footsteps hammer the stairs.

Blue.

Now I can see it is not the green uniform he wore when he first came this way, but blue. Slate-blue.

'It's not him, Mother,' Rachel says, her voice flat.

But it has to be. I made him come again by willing it. And the colours are different, so this time it will be better. I will be prepared, so the misfortune will stay away; no longer will I be Not-Louise. Hope will return and this time remain.

He crosses the grass, striding towards the house. As he passes the window, he takes off his cap and I see fair hair beneath. Only then, as Kate bursts back into the room, do I realise.

'Please don't ruin it for me.'

Kate's off up the stairs once more – 'Got to check how I look!' – leaving just Rachel staring out the window; William has slumped into his chair. As the grey-blue man raps on the door I want to cry out, but whatever I do, however hard I strain, all that comes forth is an empty rasp. Like the one Nan gave when she saw my poisoned hollowness.

And still I am nothing; the ill luck lingers. Floating all around us like the blossom that is blowing on the breeze.

THE AIR MAN

Sleepy's not the word. Unconscious more like. Sunday, I know, but even so... It's the end of the road and a circle of cottages surrounds me. I don't recognise any of them from last night, and there's nobody around to ask. I ease myself off the bike, scratching an itch under my cap and getting my breath, when an old boy appears out of one of the gardens. He looks about ninety-three, eyeing me up like I'm a German paratrooper.

'Y'alright?' he says.

'Whereabouts am I exactly?'

After a time he answers, though the words seem to take hours to move between his head and mouth. I think he's calling me uncommon – which I suppose I must be, a real sight round here – before I manage to translate his thick accent.

'Right, this is the Common! Well I'm looking for the Abreharts' house.'

He gives a sort of wheeze, like he's having a fit, though I think he's laughing.

'Abreharts! You want to be...' And I catch something about the village and church – opposite the church? – but the rest's lost on me, so I just nod my head, smile, and start back the way he was pointing. I turn right at the junction, past a little flint-clad school, and after a few hundred yards go straight ahead down a thinner road when the main one snakes round to the left. More cows and fields and, finally, a few scattered hovels and farm buildings, and a big house fronted by a high wall.

Ain't much of a place.

Can't be barely fifty people living here – and that's if they're crammed in tight. There's the church – but unless they're in that barn, there's no way they're opposite like the old boy said. Don't appear to be nothing else along the road in front, except a wall of trees that must mark the village edge. No shop, no pub, no nothing. Will have to try and retrace our steps from last night – their cottage did seem out on a limb. Curtains twitch as I back-pedal, this time following the main loop of the road as it skirts the place in an arc so wide you wouldn't know it's even there. I press on, still not sure whether this is the right way until I see a crooked old trunk at the top of a long straight that rings some bells.

I head down it – not that it's much of road, more of a farm track with hedges towering in at either side and half of bloody Norfolk growing down the middle. Definitely not built for a man on a borrowed bike.

Now my target becomes clearer: a promising-looking building on its own at the end. Seems like the trees could swallow it up any minute. Pretty enough though, all chalk and brick straight out of a picture book. Just the four of them now, she said last night, old man pegged it a year ago. In any case I'm getting ahead of myself. Got to handle the younger sister first, let her down gently once I've got something started with Rachel. And that won't be a pushover if the dance was anything to go by. Wasn't exactly falling over herself at the sight of a man in uniform like they usually are.

Not this man anyway.

I swerve and mount the hump in the centre of the track, which almost throws me off. Ain't this lot heard of proper roads? If Jerry ever does invade I don't give it long before he turns round, sick to the back teeth of all these piddling country lanes. I coast to a standstill and lean the bike against the low hedge that runs the length of the garden. Now the church is off to my right, poking up above another load of greenery – more trees than Hyde Park! If I'd kept straight on through the village I'd have been here ten minutes ago.

Never mind, best foot forward and I'm stepping on a well-worn trail across the scruffy lawn. Here goes nothing, I think, which is a stupid expression 'cause there's no way this is nothing. Might be if I didn't care what came of it, but I do. Most definitely. I can tell 'cause my heart's running fast, like someone's holding down a foot on my accelerator. I glance across as I pass the window – there's movement inside, but I can't stop in case the sight of her makes me lose the last of my nerve. I remove my cap and smooth down my hair. Don't know why I wore it – not like she's going to suddenly become all keen 'cause of what's on top of my head.

Calmly, David, as the old boy used to say when he noticed me getting in a state at the yard over something or other: slow and steady wins the race. I pause before the door – the paint's flaking away in thin slivers – sucking in a good, proper lungful of air. I relax my breathing and everything's starting to wind down until the birds start twittering and screeching, making me lose my concentration. Get on with it, man! My hand wavers before, finally, I rap my fist against the rotting wood and step back.

The world freezes for a minute – must be more like a few seconds – and there's an apologetic creaking. She's standing before me, exactly as I remembered, though if anything even prettier, if that's possible. Dark, straight hair falling down the sides of her face, that delicate slim neck, that perfect skin...

I bring my glance up, into her deadly black eyes.

'Hello,' she says. And now I can breathe again.

'Lovely day,' I say, small talk no longer seeming my strongpoint.

She bars the way impassively.

'Pass out,' I say and she gives me a funny look. 'I've got a pass out. For the afternoon.' I'm blathering, my words all over the place. 'Thought I'd say hello to your sister. And your good self, of course.'

A hint of something – a smirk? – creeps across her face and I realise my hair is flicking stupidly in the breeze. I tighten the grip on my cap – which I'm holding like an offering – holding onto for dear life.

'She's inside.'

I stand with a big gormless grin.

'You better come in.'

She turns on her heel – what a heel – and I step after her into a room I take to be both the kitchen and parlour. A wiry beanpole of a lad stares fiercely at me from the nearest of the four chairs pulled up to a large rectangular dining table. Opposite him must be the mother, but I can't make out her face 'cause she's buried it in her hands, her long greying hair dropping in front like a camouflage net. Nearly silent sounds – are they sobs? – emerge from her hidden mouth. I don't know where to look, so concentrate on the rest of the scene. On my right's some medieval-looking set-up with a big square china sink on top and bucket underneath. No taps. To my left a smouldering fireplace. My eyes take time to adjust to the gloom. No lamp overhead, no

sign of any electricity, only the light coming in at the window –
and not too much of that 'cause the sun's in the wrong place.

It ain't exactly The Ritz.

Kate slips through the door in the other corner. She's smiling
and blushing and I grin back as she fusses me down by the fire,
next to the dark-haired boy. She keeps touching her hair and
face, checking they're still there.

'Don't worry, he won't bite!' she says. 'This is Billy.'

I hold out my hand. 'Pleased to meet you, Billy.' He doesn't
reply, just glowers at the table.

'Don't mind him. He don't say much.'

'The strong, silent type, eh?' She giggles, but the lad's head
stays bowed.

'You'll have to excuse my mother, she's not feeling too good.'

For some reason I raise my voice a little, like I'm talking to
Auntie Lottie in one of her deaf moods.

'Pleased to meet you, Mrs Abrehart.'

Her eyes are all red and her cheeks soaked. Not as ancient as I
first thought; she's got a sad face streaked with worry lines, like
she's carrying the weight of the world under her silvery barnet.

'Who's this, Rachel?'

'A friend of Kate's.'

Now the old girl's looking up at me: 'Sorry 'bout the state of
everything,' she says. 'We don't get many visitors.'

'Don't worry, Mrs Abrehart – you should see the barracks
some mornings. I'm David. David Carter.' I nod and smile,
sneaking a crafty glance at Rachel, who's prodding the stove
beneath a big iron kettle.

'Would you like anything, David?' Kate asks. 'I can make you
a sandwich or...'

'I'm fine thanks. Ate in the mess. Not the greatest grub in the
world, but they try their best.'

'David's an airman, Mother.'

She mumbles something I can't make out – I sense she's not
big on conversation.

'You'll have a cup of tea though, won't you?' Kate says. She's
a pretty thing, with her blonde hair flying everywhere, but I
can't get up any real enthusiasm. Not once I saw her sister.

75

Turns out she's only seventeen too – might get strung up for that round these parts.

'Thanks. A nice cuppa would go down a treat.'

The mother's slumped her head back into her hands and the boy's started to tap his fingers on the table, all the time eyeing me up. I smile, but he gives me a dirty scowl. Kate carries over another chair from the corner of the room and sits across from me. The kettle's whistling and Rachel brings out five mismatched cups and a yellow teapot.

'You'll have to excuse the china not being a set,' she says, as she holds the strainer in one hand and the pot in the other. 'How do you like yours, Mr. Carter?'

'Call me David, please. Mr Carter don't sound right! Dark. Nice and dark. Thank-you.'

And I can feel myself blushing, 'cause I don't want her to get the wrong idea – well, I suppose I wouldn't mind – but I only meant I like a good, strong cuppa. Fortunately, with all the shadows in the room, I doubt she's noticed. She knows how to make a brew anyway: black and thick as a pint of stout, with just a dash of milk on top.

All five of us are sitting there, though there might as well be only three; the mother's off in another world and the lad would be a devil at brag, 'cause I can't read a thing in his expression. Suddenly the old girl gets up on her feet.

'Going to go and lie down, Rachel. Goodbye Mr...'

Rachel helps her out the door. I stand, but Kate gestures me back. She looks embarrassed and I can hear their footsteps on the stairs.

'Lovely to make your acquaintance, Mrs Abrehart.' I shout after them, but no reply.

The boy's still tapping away. My eyes meet his and I nod, but he don't respond – miserable little bugger – and the room is silent apart from the sound of his furious fingers. Rachel soon re-emerges, thank Christ – it's less awkward now the mother's gone, unsettling being in the same room as someone that sad.

'Sorry about her,' Rachel says. 'She's not been feeling well lately.'

'That's alright,' I say, trying to look like the whole thing's perfectly regular.

76

'So they let you out now and again, David?' Kate asks.
'If we've been good.'
'You're so brave to fly those aeroplanes.'
Rachel pipes up. 'He's not a pilot, Kate. You're a gunner aren't you?'
'That's it. I've got the tricky job at the back.' The tricky or the stupid one. Arse-end Charlie in the thick of things.
'I know that, Rachel,' Kate snaps at her. 'I meant that he's brave to go up there on those missions. Keeping us all safe.'
'Someone's got to. Might as well be me.' I'm smiling at them, though I don't suppose what I'm saying will be much comfort next time the bullets come hurtling at us from all angles – like the other night – and it looks like I'm about to become the next newly inscribed name on the list of heroic corpses.
'Well, we're grateful for what you're doing,' Kate says, her blue eyes virtually glowing. I'm a bit embarrassed, so just sit there. Out of nowhere, the lad jerks to his feet and goes to the front door.
'Where you off to, Billy?' Kate calls across, but he's gone without a word. She turns to me. 'Sorry about him, he's been like this ever since... Your uniform probably reminds him; Father was in the forces too. The army – in the last one.'
I nod. 'Don't worry, I remember what it's like being a lad – never easy round strangers. He'll get used to me when he's seen me around some more.'
Kate smiles, this seems to go down well with her – I glance across at Rachel but can't gauge her reaction one little bit. Cagey lot, these Abreharts. Can see she's going to be a tough one to crack.
'No, I'd be happy to kick a ball about with him, play a bit of cricket.'
'He don't go in much for all that. Likes wandering around the woods, collecting birds eggs, that sort of thing...'
'He'll have to give me the guided tour then! Always thought I should see a bit more nature now I'm surrounded by so much of it. Speaking of that, was wondering if you two ladies would like to get a breath of fresh air? Such a lovely afternoon – seems wrong to be stuck indoors.'

They're both replying and on their feet at the same time – Kate saying she'd love to and Rachel that she's got the dishes to wash.

'I'm a dab hand with a dishcloth. We'll soon get this lot done,' I say.

'No, you two go. I've got plenty to be getting on with. And there's Mother...'

'Thanks Rachel, I'll do them tonight. Come on David – I'll show you some of the scenery you've been missing.' Kate's smirking, shepherding me towards the door before I can think of a way to stay.

'Sure you won't come?' I say to Rachel, but she shakes her head and I know there's no way I'm going to persuade her.

Shame. A bloody shame.

'Well, thanks for the cuppa. Tell your mother I hope she soon feels better.' I'm sure she's softening, 'cause I can sense the faintest hint of a smile as she closes the door.

Outside, Kate grins up at me like a little kid. 'Let's go to the watercress beds,' and she starts leading me down an overgrown path that runs along the edge of the garden. It's narrow and dark so we go in single file, both sides bordered by vicious-looking stinging nettles. Bluish flowers cover the ground beneath the overhanging trees. Kate skips in front and every few yards turns and gives me a cheeky look. After a while we come to a meadow with a few cows – or are they bulls? – in the far corner. Some black shapes are scrabbling around in the treetops making a heck of a racket, like a bunch of strangled cats. She's leaning against the gate and, as I catch up, she laughs and grabs my waist, planting a big wet smacker on my mouth.

I kiss her back, but it don't seem right – not just the whole thing with Rachel either – so I break my lips off from hers.

'There. You hear that? Moving about in the wood.'

'Don't be silly, David,' she says, rummaging her fingers through my hair. 'It's only the rooks. We're *rarely* going to have to teach you country ways, aren't we?'

As it dawns on me she means *really* – that accent again – her hand heads south and clasps onto my arse. But as we start kissing I swear it's not just the bloody chooks or whatever they're called peering out at us from among the greenery. I step back in a bit of a fluster.

'Let's take a gander at this famous watercress, then,' I say, keen to get away sharpish.

'Somewhere else I want to show you first.'

'Alright then.'

And I hurry her over the gate, 'cause I've the funniest feeling someone's watching us.

WILLIAM

Mother was lying when she said he was coming back. I did not believe her at first, but then I saw the pushbike weaving down the drove like his did as he rode home of an evening from The Goat. Then I really did think it could be him, but only for a second. I know he cannot return because I was there when it happened.

And later, as they lowered the ropes.

I wait now, secret and still, in a place where the world has turned on its head: the sky floats a foot off the floor because the wood is awash with bluebells, which have spread themselves out across the thick-pooled shade. The flowers are so vivid – even in the deepest shadows they seem to give off their colour – yet they fade to nearly-silver where the sun sneaks through the green gaps above. They are like an army; sometimes they all point one direction, but next time you look they face the opposite way. He used to reckon if you crept up on them you could catch them ringing in the breeze. I crouch at the edge of the indigo expanse, but they are silent; the flowers know full well I am here so are staying quiet, teasing their heads before me in the breeze.

Beyond them stands my sister and the Air Man; they have no idea I am watching.

I lean against a tall, scaly elm, its grey trunk spotted with patches of mustard-yellow lichen. The skin on my ankle is all red and bubbled-up where a nettle has got it, and a big old horsefly is buzzing around my face, but I cannot swat it and make a fuss else they will realise I am here. The stink of ramsons from the clump of jagged white petals behind me overpowers the air. The soil feels damp and heavy as I squeeze a handful in my fist – it is hard to breathe in its mouldy earthiness because the garlic smell around me shoots up my nose, making me want to sneeze.

A brown butterfly flits about the glade; I keep losing him in the blur of colours and patched sunlight. He lands on top of one of the nearby flower-clusters but still the tiny bells do not ring out at the disturbance. His thin speckled wings unfold, rich brown with creamy yellow spots round the edge and pin-pricks set among dark circles like eyes. Not his real eyes: they must be at the end of the feelers that come out the top of his head. He turns around and brings his wings together – underneath they are paler, patterned like bark – then spies me and flicks into the blue.

Kate and the Air Man are far enough away now, so I grab a dock leaf and rub its damp-dark over the sting. This is not the first time I have sat here in secret watching a man and a lady – the half-sounds of their talking reminds me.

Only before, it was not my sister and the Air Man.

I am waiting for the bluebells, to stop myself from thinking about Laura, who has not been gone more than a few days. Two voices drift out of the trees as I sit. I do not know who it can be so slide onto my stomach, settling among the ramsons. As the sounds get nearer, I recognise the man.

Him.

Peering through the stems I see they have stopped at the far end of the glade. I hope they do not realise I am here because his eyes are sharp as a sparrow hawk's and he notices the slightest movement. I inch my body into the leaves to avoid detection; doing this gives me an idea of how the flowers twist their heads without anyone knowing.

The lady is Mrs Morley – Tom's mother – though I cannot think why she would be here with him. I strain my ears to catch what the pair of them are saying but the sounds keep getting muddled with the rooks chuntering above and all I can make out is a mess of cries and shouts.

Her face is angry and so red that, as her mouth moves, I think she might even go up in flames. He turns his back on her like he is having a wordless conversation with himself and then, after what must be at least a minute or two, says something else, before crunching away through the shadows.

She slumps into the bluebells and through the sobbing I can hear her calling his name. She keeps on, but he does not reappear. After a while, her blaring dies down and she just lies there with her face to the soil. I rise noiselessly and slink home.

When I get back, he has a scowl like a storm cloud and is raking hell out of the vegetable patch, even though there are no weeds left to lift. He does not so much as glance at me as I walk past and go inside. Later, as we sit eating tea Kate asks:

'What you been up to, Billy?'

'Nothing.'

'Liar,' she says. 'You reek of stinking onions!'

And I cannot trust myself to look across at him in case my eyes give anything away.

This time, though, it is my sister who is lying. She was not with Audrey and Rose last night, but with the Air Man. He has her leant against the gate; his face is all red and he is making her grab him because he wants to put it in her.

They are all BLOODY LIARS, even Rachel; she knew about the Air Man too, because she walked back with Kate and him last night – though at least she is at home now, so he cannot put it in her as well. But I promised, so my sisters must not lie down with no one. He would be raging if Kate followed Rachel and had a baby, even though he loved little Laura too much. And if Kate's belly is to swell I will have to be like him, because I am their only brother and the last Abrehart man left. Besides, the Air Man is an idiot, and he must not make Kate become like when Rachel said she was expecting. She must not become a LITTLE WHORE.

The pair of them have started across the meadow and he looks scared – trying to scamper away, even – as the bullocks come for a closer view of him in his stupid blue uniform.

STUPID BLOODY IDIOT, THEY WILL NOT HURT YOU!

Above me, the elms sit heavy with dirty great bundles of sticks where the rooks have their nests. They fly about like giant bats and are chuntering away louder than usual – louder even than before – perhaps because they think the Air Man and my sister are after their eggs.

CARNT, CARNT they scream out. Like when we were in his house the final time and he was rasping. He did not finish – and I did not properly get his words – but he must have meant that the unknown soldier cannot be with Rachel. Or else seen ahead to the Air Man sniffing around, even though Kate had not laid eyes on him back then and the war had yet to start.

That must be what he meant.

CARNT. CARNT.

Their cawing taunts me and, though I promised to watch out for my sisters every single hour of the day, to protect them at all times because I am the head of the family now, I cannot bring myself to follow any further. I curl into a ball and lean back against the trunk's roughness.

Snot dribbles down my face like dirty cuckoo spit, while above me the rooks in their Parliament sit in mocking judgement.

MR MARSHAM

Appraising the burgeoning shoots of barley in the early evening light, I am transported back to that exceptional September day, even though more than a decade has since passed. It is a scene that will remain forever imprinted in my mind. Indelible, like a name – the thing, in the end, it all comes down to. What else is there? It struck me rather poignantly outside the church this morning as the three of them paused, so awkward, by his make-shift marker, not sure exactly what it was they ought to be doing. The younger girl was on her knees, fair and healthy look-ing, her well-turned calf framed against the green of the grave. She's in service with her sister at the Hall, though that one is different again: just like him, all willowy and dark, with the same aquiline nose. The boy's the spit of his father in colouring too. Already some of his height but, as yet, none of the grand physique. He's still young though, all his filling-out to come – a good way to go before he matches the one who seeded him.

He cut a fine figure, John Abrehart. Tall and lean yet strong as a shire horse – a prize specimen.

The men were loading hay when the idea first came to me. I was taking advantage of the late summer reprise we were enjoy-ing and had walked up to ask Horton a question pertaining to the arrangements for the next Tuesday Market. Looking across – from this very spot – towards where they worked in the far corner, I could not take my eyes off the vista before me: like something in a painting or out of Greek myth. The field glasses were in my pocket so I watched them all for a time through the shimmering heat haze, hidden from their sight behind the hedge-row; they had not the slightest inkling I was there.

He had his shirt off. None of the others did, only him, so he stood out – a beacon in a sea of bent, grey-clothed beggars. The sun caught his hair, making it glister in the late afternoon light as he plucked the bales, like they were without substance, and pitched them into the cart. The muscles in his tanned arms and bull-neck were taut, his face red, his sweat-sheened torso mag-nificent: the antithesis of the pale wraith he was to become, crumpled at the foot of those stairs.

Eventually, one of the men must have noticed me, and Horton scampered over. A blessing perhaps, because if he hadn't I would have stood there for hours, hypnotised by that classical tableau.

Rosamond takes quite the interest in the four who are left, dropping round parcels of extra food and whatnot. Her civic duty she calls it – a wife with a husband helping a widow not so fortunate – but she doesn't need to dress it up for my benefit. I know she feels obliged, as do I: in my case, particularly where the boy is concerned. I don't like to think of him cast adrift in the world, so have promised a permanent position when his schooling ends. As to what practical use he'll be – quiet as the grave and perhaps a little soft in the head – I'm not too sure, though there's an intensity about him I hope will apply in similar measure to his labours. Silence must be another quality he has inherited from his father, because John Abrehart certainly knew how to hold his tongue.

When I put the proposal to him it was within his power to make me a laughingstock, or worse, though I am not naive; he did not keep his counsel out of any propriety towards me. He knew well enough that I needed say only one word to bring about the end of him so far as employment and lodging were concerned. All this, of course, I had weighed up when I made the approach, balancing the probability of disclosure against the alternatives. Him rejecting the deal in no uncertain fashion was, I thought, the most likely outcome. I would have respected that and said no more about the matter, providing he could assure me of his discretion. As to him agreeing, I had heard enough idle talk concerning his reputation to make me think there was a chance.

Quite correctly, he had certain questions as to the scope of his expected duties and the limits of his liability, but once I assured him on these matters he calmly accepted my terms. We shook hands and I told him the deal would begin, in earnest, when I had finalised the arrangements, and remuneration would cease as soon as a satisfactory conclusion had been reached. Despite the fact discussions had taken place over a period of months, I was still not sure as to the other party's willingness to proceed once the situation progressed beyond the hypothetical. One thing was clear, however, even at this early stage: I myself possessed few doubts as to the suitability of the plan. Yes, the question of breeding remained – a detail more than outweighed by the strapping appearance of the sire concerned – but I was confident any such issues that might arise could be positively influenced and nurtured in due course, thereby eradicating any potential future problems.

So it began, with no complaints from any involved. However, it soon became apparent that proceedings would have to continue longer than initially planned – the swift satisfaction I had blithely assumed to be a formality not forthcoming. I was aware these things can take a while, but after three months grew concerned with the lack of progress. However, the participants were keen to keep pressing ahead and finish what had been started so I agreed to a further extension, which I assumed would be adequate to allow a satisfactory conclusion. Regrettably, after the revised season had passed, we were no closer to our initial goal; I had to disengage John Abrehart from our arrangement and resign myself to disenchantment. Naturally, my wife was upset beyond words, because I know she had wanted success, as much, if not more than myself. Yet I had to remain adamant.

'Rosamond, this ends now,' I insisted over her incessant tears, smarting at the venom in her voice as she shouted her dissent.

'If you won't put a stop to it, I will,' I said.

'You! How?'

'I can see to him. Make no mistake.'

There was one silver lining to the disruption: I knew now the fault did not lie with me. Yes, our intimacies over the years had become increasingly infrequent, but liaisons of that nature had taken place on occasion (though I admit the encounters provided me with little satisfaction). No, when even a well-practised stallion like John Abrehart could make no headway, some underlying barrenness on the part of my wife seemed the likeliest cause.

He returned to mere horticultural tasks and I busied myself with the intricacies of the Estate. Yet something inexplicable had shifted and thereafter an awkwardness existed when I came upon him in one of the fields, or when encountering his family at church. Perhaps this is an outcome I should have accounted for, though I did not expect such irrational emotions – the most unwanted consequence of Rosamond's reaction – to intrude

86

upon matters of the home. Over the years we had reached an unspoken understanding about the boundaries of our relationship, of what we each expected from the other; yet this interruption seemed to throw that frail equilibrium into turmoil. Rosamond could barely bring herself to speak civilly to me any more, and I too found it hard to look upon her in the same light. She began to avoid the house, taking walks through the woods and across the meadow for inordinate periods of time, the meal not ready on the dining table when I returned each day. This unsavouriness persisted for over a year, until finally she made her peace and implored me to return the status quo to its previous state. I was happy to agree as I was sure our discord was becoming apparent to certain, more inquisitive, members of the village – a situation I could not countenance: the Colonel would not have approved of the manager of his Estate being involved in something so unsightly. I decided the moment had arrived to put aside any personal delicacies on my part and so, for a time, recommenced my conjugal duties – if not with aplomb then at least without quite the usual dread. However, still no progress occurred, and I was on the verge of admitting that our mutual hope would have to remain an unattainable asset. Indeed, I found myself rushing back from a meeting with fellow livestock breeders one Friday evening to outline a path forward, because her unrealistic expectations weighed increasingly on my conscience.

Guttural grunts greeted me as I entered the house. I strained to listen from the kitchen, immutable for what seemed like an age before making my way to the dining room door. There she lay on the table and, although her head was hidden underneath his naked, iron-hard body, I could picture the ecstasy etched across her face. His rump was magnified as my eyes followed its rise and fall through the thickly glazed panels: Michelangelo's David gloriously rendered in flesh.

When some weeks later she announced she was with child I feigned surprise, the sight of the two of them singed into my memory: *His seed shall remain for ever, and his glory shall not be blotted out.* Despite the deception, I was delighted we would both soon possess our most-coveted desire. Though, of course, the irony of the outcome's impermanence is not lost on me.

She's before me now, her ebony locks made animate by the breeze as she skips along the headland of the field: Ruth Marsham, at least for a few years more, till marriage robs me even of her name.

The daughter I was destined never to have.

WILLIAM

If the weather holds, what is left of the light will linger till late. My eye is on the woodcock who has been making his fat-bellied flights up and down the ride out the far end of the meadow this past month, uttering his croak and squeak: he must be guarding a nest somewhere. Some people reckon a goldcrest will hitch on a woodcock's back like a miniature pilot, and he once saw one carrying its chick between its legs as it flapped away from him through the trees. I would love to see that, though I will settle for spying the hen bird squatting like a pile of brown leaves among the litter – her egg shall definitely go in my woodland box, despite her waterbird beak.

And, if I am very lucky, he will be in his house again. Waiting for me.

Mother is facing the flowerbed, sucking in the air's matted scent like a slow-hovering night-moth. She does not notice as I head onto the path through the trees, fixed to her spot as I step along its surface. Soon tall nettles rise and cut out my view; they absorb the sounds of the open so I can no longer hear the corn bunting that is jangling from somewhere up the drove. Arriving at the gate I swing myself over in one smooth motion, the movement natural as taking a breath. The cattle trot slowly back in my direction – head-for-home time again – dragging their hooves like shovels. They do not even stop to piss, letting it splash at their feet in stinking great puddles. A brown cow comes snorting over for a closer look and I stroke her matted flank; she shakes her head then ambles farmwards with the others. They never tire of forever doing the same thing and I like them for that: every day identical to the one before, which is how I want to be, never forgetting a single word he said. Because if I change too much it will all become lies and I will never be able to make it go back.

It must be after eight by now – I find it tricky to keep track of time as I do not have a watch and the clock on the church stopped turning when the war began. Gnats spin round me in loose circles. The air hangs heavy with rain and I think a storm might be building. Mr Croxton says we could do with some precipitation, because now is a vital time for the crops to get a good soaking and there has not been a real drop for two weeks.

I carry on, past the place where it happened, which lies in thick shade. If a person were to pass, they would think the trees there just sprout more thickly. When you know, like me, you can make out what is hidden, because something is not right with how that vague shape sits among the gloom, and the way the light clings about the branches.

Pressing on across the meadow, I reach the gap where the ride was cut out, way back, for the rich lot to go out fox-hunting and the like. This will be the best place to spy on the woodcock flapping above – now the colour is dipping he should soon come grunting along. I take up a stick and beat a way in front; nettles reign here again because there are not enough spare men left at the farm to keep on top of such jobs. I strike the bristled stems and they flop, though I know however hard I hack, new ones will rise in their place.

I straddle a fallen log that bridges the ride, and lie back. My face points to the sky, cooler now with the way the wind is swaying the branches. Darkness is creeping up fast, grey clouds have covered the sun's earlier false promise of through-the-night day. I try to think about him and me together but nothing comes, only an emptiness pressing on my skull. A jenny-wren scolds from the dense undergrowth and soon her buzzing body bobs into sight; she tires after a while and sneaks back below the green-dark, leaving me alone on the log, quiet but for the strengthening gusts. Above me, the gnats continue to loop in never-ending jerks.

Movement ahead: I lie silent and rigid. A doe inches into the ride, nibbling at the dampness. She senses something amiss but the breeze blows against her, covering my scent as she comes slowly closer. Flies crawl along my arm, but I do not move an inch. Now she is stretching up her neck, sniffing the air: suddenly she twigs and notices my outline against the trunk, flashing her dull white arse up the track and vanishing back from where she came.

Moisture flicks my face, though at first I am not sure if it is rain or just tree-wet. Another droplet. Then big, laden splashes.

I open my mouth and try to drink as it starts to sheet down. I have no jacket but do not care – I like the feeling as the sky sweats onto me, the cool wetness stinging my face. The birds seem excited at the prospect too: a chiffchaff begins its stop-start song and a chaffinch lets out its raindrop call.

Thunder snarls in the distance, and the pressure gathered lead-heavy in the air these past few nights is released.

The rain tumbles hard; soon I will be drenched. The wood-cock will not make his special display in this – and even if he does I will not be able to find where his nest lies – so I rise from the log and begin hurrying back. Lightning streaks the wood ahead. I should not stay out in the open, so veer beneath the cover of the closest trees, brambles scratching my arms until I am up the three ivy-hidden steps and through the half-hanging door to his house. I head past the stairs, not looking up even once, before sinking against the fireplace.

Outside the air explodes.

The space can barely be called a room since the woods started their work; a tiny sycamore is pushing its way up through the floor, and fresh deathwatch holes pinprick the rafter above me. I tap to try and make them emerge – like beating the ground to charm worms to the surface – but my fingertips make little sound against the backdrop of rumbling and rain. I do this for an age, but no heads poke their way out. My eyes become used to the twilight and I spot details I missed when I arrived: a dog fox has been in the corner and marked the place as his, and beside the window a bloated bumblebee sits shivering on the rotten sill. The single chair magnifies the room's loneliness and makes my anger rise – I should stamp and smash its mocking spindles, but I cannot bring myself.

Is he there? I ought to check, even though climbing those stairs is not something I like to do. Outside the downpour de-scends, soaking the backs of my calves as I hesitate in the doorway. I focus on the flimsy floorboards in front of me, care-ful not to look straight up above my head.

Noiseless movements, snail-stepping past the gaping holes un-til I have almost reached the top. I think my foot forward onto the landing, pulling my body behind. A loose board threatens a groan that never comes and, relieved, I edge across the space.

At first I do not see him, only his mess scattered on the floor.

Now, though, I can make his white shape out, tucked atop the rafter by the window. He cannot be very old, which would explain why he has no nest – he has found this place to roost during the day, practising his hunting at night. Next year he will get himself a mate, perhaps. He sits steady now, one black eye flicking open in that heart-shaped face to check what I am up to – a beautiful cream-bellied ghost. When I watch him quartering the meadow he does not fly like other birds with deliberate sharp beats, paddling instead through the air as if it were water, stirring the currents with his round-edged wings.

His body is so slender I think he must be a man. The females are fatter since they have to squeeze the eggs from their backsides.

Both black depths are now blinking wide: two endless hollows directed towards me. Only a screech owl, but still so difficult to hold that gaze because the blackness – and this place – reminds me. I crouch against the wall, his eyes following my every movement; I pull my knees to my chest and breathe hard, because I do not want to feel that way again.

Must think of better days.

At last, something which has not come to me for the longest time, almost before remembering: shapes and senses that whip out from old places, all tears and hunger, crying and laughter.

His hands dwarfing mine and rough with bark-skin, but no ants crawling up them like on the apple tree which is their sky-ladder. I climb too, until wasps hover with sharp backs, yellow and black, so that I am falling, then running in broken circles.

'Don't be scared,' he says, 'Only makes them worse.' But I cannot stop for all the buzzing.

Now plucking me aloft and wiping the red that gashes my shin where the branch caught. Me wheeze-wheezing so I cannot hear nothing.

'Stop wailing, William, and I'll show you something special.'

Three dirty feather-things craning upright in the barn.

Hisssssssss.

'Look and listen, but don't touch – their beaks are sharp.'

'You are hisssssssss,' they say together.

Ghostflight. Dead mouse dropping into biggest mouth. My leg stings so I cry out, only too loud. Just the three screeching shapes now, angry and agape.

Shush, rub it away. Piggybacking down the long straight, drowsy in the dusk.

'Why do they live there?'

'Because they love barns,' he says. 'That's why they're called barn owls.'

I slump into the half-light, drifting in and out of sleep as the thunder ignites the air overhead. Only partially aware of the world, I squint at the dust and mess strewn across the floor, a pile of blackish pellets beneath where he perches. I pick at the closest, all smooth and furry – the rat and mice fur he cannot digest – crumbling it into my palm to study its contents: tiny mashed skulls and bones.

Away again, dreaming of that pale-pink bill opening and closing; he talks to me in screeches, only I do not understand a word he says.

I feel myself sinking into the damp, smothered by the hush of the house and the heavy scent of nettles. Almost as soon as my head hollows out a place for itself I am off again and dreaming:

We are trapped in a thicket and I cannot move. Spiked shoots wrap my legs, inching their way to my waist. They are about him too but he has his knife and, as he hacks at them, they fall. He stands strong, freeing himself from the tangle, and strides in my direction, swiping into the undergrowth as he comes. When he reaches me the blade slices effortlessly through the stems and their ends sizzle, as if alight. He slashes back the worst and picks me up with one arm. Then, carrying me, he is off again – the creeping branches cannot get a hold and it feels like we are floating above them.

'There,' he says and I spot it on the ground in a neat nest of dry thorns, ruby-red and plump. Its sides move in and out – tick-tick, tick-tock – in time with the tapping of the deathwatches.

'It's my heart,' he whispers.

'Why haven't you got it?'

'I don't need one.'

93

And the magic piper starts playing and in the dream I see he is not a nightingale, but a tiny man who weaves among the trunks before us – always before us – until he is lost from our sight in the shadows.

My eyelids open and the room is reborn, dark but for the moonlight angling onto the pale shape above: awake and alert he shuffles on the rafter, stretching skywards. He turns his speckled grey-brown back so it faces me, darker here at rest than when he flies cream-gold in the evening sun. His wings hang down past his squared-off tail like curved blades. He swivels his head for one last look and propels himself into the night.

Rain still machine-guns what remains of the roof – though now not as fast as before – and a narrow stream trickles through a crack in the ceiling. If I miss him in the meadow when I walk back, I know I will be able to find him here again.

Down the broken stairs and out the doorway to the wet world, a gleam covering everything and stream-sounds filling my head. The trees hug the house tight, because they do not want it back to being a people-place. I slither through the undergrowth, cold dripping down my neck and under my shirt, pleased when I reach the open, away from all the water cascading off the leaves; the rain has almost stopped and the rumbling is diminished.

The empty meadow is murky and mysterious, so different to the day with its glimmering grass and yellow-blazing buttercups. I head towards the ride – perhaps the woodcock will do his fat-bodied flight after all, now the rain is stopping. I still might be able to pick his silhouette against the western sky or the uncovering moon – its glow turns the clouds silver as wisps of vapour drift across the three-quarter circle.

Distant thunder growls, this time a constant drone, not the earlier violent drum roll. Still miles off, but I am aware of its gradual approach. Drizzle flicks the dark turf where an army of slugs trail – any hedgehogs snuffling around will be in for a right feast. Tea seems a lifetime ago and I feel ravenous again; I shall have to find some supper-bread when I return.

I hope Rachel does not sit worrying over me being out – she should know I can look after myself by now. It will be better if she does not realise, because if she discovers I have been out this late she will nag me about having to get up for school, with it being Monday in the morning; Mother will not notice and Kate is too busy dreaming of the Air Man to concentrate on anything else. I cannot be certain if he stuck it in her earlier this afternoon after they left me by the bluebells, but I think something must have happened because she was acting all funny and giggly when she came back without him for tea. He should leave my sister alone, though – we do not need him wobbling down the drove on his bicycle like a circus clown.

I hope his air plane gets shot, that will put a stop to his games. Not that I want the Germans to invade. Then they will be after my sisters too, which must not happen. Mr Croxton told us on Friday how our men in the BEF – which is the British Expeditionary Force that Kate says Tom is in – are holding firm and doing their utmost to hold back the Germans from heading closer this way. He read out to us what Mr Churchill said last week, about not only winning the battle but winning the war; about being men of valour, and how we all need to take every single step, make every last inch of effort, to help ensure the Germans are beaten back. So, even though we must be at least twenty miles here from the beaches where they may land, I will be ready to do my bit for King and Country. And, if the worst does happen, this is where I will make my stand to protect Mother and Kate and Rachel – out here in these woods like Robin Hood in the stories. Even if they will not give me a gun, because I am not old enough, I can still use his catapult and knife to pick them off one by one.

The sound grows louder. Not thunder, I realise, but a bomber passing overhead. Hearing it makes the hairs on the back of my neck stand on end; it sounds too low to be German, it must be one of ours. I imagine them on their way out to batter the Jerries, and feel proud of the brave crew inside until I realise that the Air Man – what a grinning idiot – might be on board. Even so, I cross my fingers and take back the thought about them being brought down. I hope only he gets it and the rest make it home all right; I will settle for him just getting wounded, as long as they send him away to another base far from here, where he cannot trouble my sisters no more.

The hum of the bomber is everywhere, bringing the meadow to life so my stewed feet swarm with hundreds of skittering daddy-long-legs. Finally my eyes make out a distant, stiff-winged gliding way above the trees. I watch its stubby shape pass before the mist-white moon clouds, insignificant up there in the endless night sky. Harmless for now, despite its angry low drone.

And the death it will deliver like rain.

THE AIR MAN

The ground becomes a memory once you're airborne, hard to square with all those tiny, mishmashed fields and hedgerows that seem so big when you're cycling past. It's different again up here in the moonlight and I almost think I'm dreaming, though there's not too many opportunities to nod off with the throb of the engines and drunken reek of fuel filling your head. Not to mention the freezing bloody cold and the other lot taking pot-shots left, right and centre. Even so, it helps to get a bit of shut-eye when the opportunity arises, else you're in for a long night.

Flying by day's different again: you can see cows and sheep standing around like they don't realise there's a war on – though why should it matter to them, they'll end up on the dinner table whoever comes out on top? I can't make out their silhouettes now – probably hunkered under a haystack somewhere if they've got any sense.

From two thousand feet nature's stopped dead in its tracks, though when you're down wandering those little lanes in the dark there's enough rustling among the trees to suggest all sorts of funny business. Give me Acton High Street any night of the week – I'd much rather handle some cocky drunk staggering out of The George than a startled poacher jumping me from the bushes. Still at least there's no danger of getting run over here, not like back home where most nights some stupid bugger's guaranteed to step in front of a car, or off a train platform, 'cause they can't find their way in the blackout.

The weather's cleared after its earlier blow. Shame it didn't keep up – wouldn't have minded an early night, or a swift jaunt to the pub. At least this has spared me a ribbing from the blokes about Kate. Just jealousy – they were drooling over her when she came over at the dance last night; they'd all leap at the chance if she flashed one of her big smiles in their direction. I tried to explain the problem – about Rachel – to Jack this morning, but he couldn't cotton on to what I was saying. Well, use the little blonde for practice, was the best he could come up with, and I certainly can't accuse her of being shy at rehearsals. Forward's not the word – she was the one egging me on this afternoon, not more than half an hour after I'd been sat in their cheerless front room with the mother sobbing and the little brother giving me evils. I went along with it 'cause she's certainly a looker. But something didn't feel right and, as her face bobbed above me, her cheeks all flushed and her mouth open in a little grin, I couldn't help substitute her image with that of her sister's, which soon made me lose my focus. I don't think the place we were in helped: a dingy old cottage rotting away in the middle of the woods.

'What's the matter,' she said, 'you want me to do it different?'

'No, it's not you.'

She began grinding away on top, but all I could concentrate on was some faint bloody tapping sound coming from the walls, so I pushed her off. She seemed all set to start crying and I wasn't feeling too clever about the whole thing, seeing how she was making such an effort. You've got to sort this out, David, I thought, wondering whether it wouldn't be as bad if I didn't have to look directly into her face.

So I flipped her over and, though I was still picturing Rachel, the guilt hit me less hard and I managed to get going and finish the job. She seemed chirpier too, squeezing my hand as we walked, in silence, the rest of the way back.

I can't go through that again. Can't handle the way those puppy-dog eyes stare up at me like I'm the answer to everything. No easy way out, though – I'll just have to end it. She's a sweet girl but I shouldn't have let it go so far. Worst thing is, when I do break it off it's not like I'll be able to pop round the next day for a crack at Rachel – and I'm hardly likely to bump into her in the street somewhere.

'Come to see if you fancy a bit of a roll in the hay now I've finished with your sister.'

'Thanks, David, thought you'd never ask!'

I wish there was a way I could get Rachel on her own, but I've the feeling she keeps herself hidden away deliberately – a crying shame 'cause the world deserves a good look at her; though I suppose it's no bad thing, as some other crafty sod would soon snap her up were she out on show. If I could only see her alone for a proper chat I'd be able to weigh up my chances; I'm sure I sensed something between us last night at the dance – just needs the opportunity to develop.

The four of them are below us somewhere now. A black box-ful of peaceful sleepers dreaming their dreams, unaware we're gliding above, off to spread some mayhem across the sea.

I picture Rachel stretched out on the bed wearing next to nothing, those long lashes fluttering in her sleep, her mouth murmuring something I can't quite hear. Her eyes flick wide, staring up at me cradled in the back of the Wellington – bigger, blacker and more beautiful than anything else down there in the real world.

'I want you, David,' she whispers, beckoning me towards her. And I'm ready to bail, to fall endlessly into those dark depths.

'Wake up, sleeping beauty!'

I snap up with a start, banging my bonce in the process.

'Just resting me eyes, Sarge.' I smile back at him and he gives me a gap-toothed grin. We're high now and the cold's started to hit, the fumes filling my head. No time left to dream, David Carter. 'Cause if you want to ever wake again in your own bed – or, please God, Rachel's for that matter – you've got to pray for a gallon of good fortune to hold together this botch-up of metal and canvas.

Taller shapes below mark another identical village, its round-towered church circled by a cluster of sloping cottages. Now there's a glint, a still-watered lake bordered by yet more woods and fields. I wouldn't mind catching another forty winks, but it's too late, the land's already falling away and the moon highlights a finish line of white horses breaking onto the distant beach: the last of England, the point of no return.

The place you realise you're going to need every scrap of courage you've got saved up to make it back from the fighting, the flak, and the fear.

RACHEL

Kate grunts in her sleep, anchoring me to my bed as, vainly, I try to drift off. Somewhere way above I hear the rumble of an aeroplane. Starlight sneaks through the thin gauze of curtain; I can make out my sister's restless outline in the grey-black gloom. Too many thoughts are shearing off inside me, holding me back from sleep.

How is Rachel? The words in Tom's letter that asked about me – I can't get them away from my head.

Please let him be all right. Let his silence be because the army won't allow them to be in touch, what with the fighting and all the secret preparations they must be making. Besides, anything awful and they would've contacted Mrs Morley, wouldn't they?

Next time he comes home I won't waste the chance – I will make it better. My father shan't come between us from where he festers – he'll not ruin things for us again like he did before.

Completely awake now, I sense a change in the air – the breeze seems suddenly fresher, more alive. The thought makes me smile, though only my blanket-hid sister's here to witness. If you are up there, God, please keep Tom safe so we can have a second chance. Please let life go back to how it should've been. Too much has been taken away already – surely we deserve some happiness?

I promise: what we have will be special and pure. Like it was before *he* had to spoil it.

The room's still steaming, my pyjamas stuck fast to my sweat-beaded skin; the storm hasn't managed to disperse any of the night's stuffiness. Kate's sighs fill the dark and her arm sprawls over the side of the bed at an ugly, twisted angle.

Her David might be nothing like Tom, but at least she's able to have him.

Rising, my eyes now accustomed to the room's moon-washed glow, I slip from under the sheet and pad barefoot down the stairs. Air piles in as I part the curtains and open the kitchen window; I pour myself some water from the jug and sit at the table. Even though midnight must be approaching, the room has an odd radiance, an unreal tint that makes it seem a strange copy of the place it passes for during daylight. I remember sitting like this in Tom's kitchen, while Mrs Morley was away visiting her sister in Norwich. That's where I told him I was expecting. He looked worried but took my hands in his and assured me not to be frightened, he'd see everything worked out right.

'I don't go breaking a promise,' he said. 'We'll just have to get married, won't we?'

Something glistens on the table – one of Mother's thin darning needles. She leaves them carelessly around the house when she's mending clothes – often I find them pushed into a cushion, it's one of the superstitions she clings to. You're supposed to picture a missing object while you repeat the phrase, then pin something soft and wait for the thing to turn up.

Tom's lost to me now, I realise, scooping the needle between my thumb and index finger, all the time imagining his frightened eyes searching me out from those foreign fields.

'I pin the Devil.'

I speak quietly. No cushion to hand so I roll back my sleeve and jab the needle into the top of my wrist. It stings as it pierces my skin but I don't care about the pain. I push down so the shaft pokes up like the Maypole on the Common, wobbling its head from side to side. I withdraw its sharpness and trail the point along my arm: the skin parts and a gentle sea breaks through. I stop and press harder.

'I pin the Devil.'

Louder this time, as I'm saying it imagining Tom marching down the drove and back into my arms. 'Look at you,' he'll laugh, lifting me up and twirling me around.

All at once I feel stupid. The sight of the jutting metal makes me queasy, so I yank it out. A fat drop of grey blood starts to seep – I can't make out colours properly in this quarter-light – and, angry with myself, I flick the needle onto the ashes of the fire.

Now you're joining Mother with her strangeness.

I dip a finger into the glass and smooth it over my punctured skin, diluting the spreading darkness to nothing. The bleeding won't stop so I wet it again, and this time the smudge on my fingertip clouds the glass's contents.

A rattling outside startles me and I grab the poker from next to the fire. Someone's at the front door. Tucked against the chimney, I hold the heavy iron stick in front of my chest and ready my body to strike, my breathing shallow and fast. Footsteps clonk the floor and a tall figure emerges through the doorway's darkness. For a moment, my mind wonders whether it could be Tom and I gasp, dropping the poker onto the hearth, only just missing my foot. The shape stumbles into the patch of moonlight, knocking the glass, its tinted water cascading over the table's edge like a waterfall.

'William, you clumsy oaf.' It comes out firm but quiet – I don't want to make any more of a row and wake Mother and Kate.

He grabs a tea towel and starts to mop the pool that has formed on the table.

'Where on earth you been? It must be almost midnight.'

He grins his I'm-sorry face as I lean across to help him, though however hard we seem to rub, tiny beads of water still coat the tabletop.

'Don't go running up to bed. I want a word.' And he stops before he can disappear from the room, sprawling himself down, all legs and gangly arms, into a chair.

'You shouldn't be out this late. There's a war on – anything could have happened.'

He sniffs a little snort, which I ignore.

'Don't you think we've got enough to worry about without you falling into a ditch somewhere and breaking your leg? Or worse, falling underneath a German bomb. Besides, it's Monday tomorrow – you've got school.'

I try and remember the sound of him in my head, but it's getting hard after all these wordless months. Next time he decides to talk – if he ever does – his voice might have broken and I shan't recognise it at all.

'You won't do it again, will you?'

He smiles silently, and I realise I can't stay cross with him for long. He rises and removes his boots in that comical way he has, then saunters up the stairs. We understand each other, I think, even if I am the only one ever doing any talking. The room's shadows have drawn themselves close, yet a sudden thought shines out at me with the clarity of daylight, and I realise why my brother has become this way:

Sometimes it's best not to talk about the sad things, the things that have been lost. Then there still might be a chance you've got it all wrong, that they haven't really happened.

Slumping, I let the dreaming wash over me, tracing Tom's name in the droplets that remain on the table's surface with my blood-smeared finger. I will find you, my love, and it won't be long; when you come home we'll be together again, just like we were meant to. And even if the world can never be as good as it was, we shan't ever forget and will return to that place where we created something so precious.

His name fades as below it I write:

L O V E R

As I watch, the water-trail evaporates and the letters transform. For a second, before they disappear entirely from view, I see a different word spelled out clear as anything:

L A U R A

And my eyes are nothing but tears.

MRS MORLEY

It's a good morning for drying – a relief because I've all the Marshams' washing to finish and their Ruth is back for the week. He picked the girl up from Lynn station yesterday morning after church – her school has a different half-term to here. A welcome distraction for Her Ladyship because it can't be easy stuck in such a big old house with only that cold-hearted husband for company, his beady eyes always measuring you up like you're livestock. No wonder she insists I call her Rosamond, even though it changes nothing and I'm still her glorified skivvy: she's desperate for anything to make her feel less alone.

I can see why she took so to *him* – he would have treated her proper, made her experience things she never thought possible. He definitely had that effect on me. I felt it the first time he told me how beautiful I was. You silly sod, John Abrehart, I said, but he kept giving me that stare and soon we were lying together. It was inevitable once he'd decided that I was the one he wanted. No guilt hit me, even though perhaps it should have. Just pure need, because it had been too long and my husband had never made me feel that way – not even before he went away whole and came back broken, full of bitterness.

Then, all of a sudden, there was John, so different again, his eyes glistening with sadness and longing after everything he'd been through, needing my comfort to satisfy his hurt. What could I do?

I'm sure Rosamond senses the awkwardness that sits between us, but does she understand its root? I don't believe she ever saw us together – and he certainly had no reason to tell – but she must have noticed the way I looked at him, or how cut up I was at the funeral. Just like she was. I watched her sneak out after the service, making the cardinal sin of abandoning her husband as he chatted to the Colonel. No doubt he'd have given her the silent treatment for weeks after that little slight.

I stir the teapot – I'm no good till my first morning cup – and sit in the triangle of early morning light that's squeezing through the window. I shouldn't blame Rosamond, the fault was mine for being so blind: for not realising sooner that I wasn't enough.

But you only see what you want to, and for that I hold up my hands. Perhaps all the secrecy surrounding our meetings made me immune to any odd behaviour on his part. I never dreamed he was carrying on behind my back, had no idea I wasn't the only other woman.

It's not just the pair of us looking at life through a veil, though. I used to wonder if the whole village chose to ignore the evidence right in front of them because they lacked the imagination – were too bound up by their own mundaneness. They couldn't possibly understand what it's like to live so close to the edge: the constant, unbearable thrill that you could fall at any minute. Like Betty Heckleton next door, too scared of the now to admit there has to be something more than loneliness and regret. That was me once – every day dying a drudge's death as my husband sat raging at life's injustice. Then John came, and in that moment I knew: I mustn't let it take me as well, because I craved something more. Even then, back when it started, I understood the wrongness, but there was nothing I could do to make it stop. It felt so good I wanted it to carry on for ever, even if it did mean cheating Louise Abrehart of what I was feeling, and cheating my husband of what he thought was his right.

I don't care about any of that; I'm not ashamed and wouldn't have ever stopped it, because I didn't have the power to. The decision was part of a force bigger than all of us. A force that wouldn't let such things ever become real and in the world if they were so wrong.

I pour my tea, watching the leaves sludge the strainer: black to save the bother of milk. I still shouldn't have said it, though. I could've shared him; it would be better than this. Than not having anything.

On the table in front of me is the photograph. Nothing hardly to it, but the only one of him I possess; I took it from a drawer in their kitchen when I went to help Louise and the girls prepare the spread after his funeral. He's in uniform – two other soldiers either side of him – staring straight into the lens.

Straight into my soul.

Was wrong of me to take it, I know, but I had to look upon him again, was still in a state after him storming off like that.

We needn't have finished on such terms, not when everything had carried along so easy, so good, for all that time. Those glorious summer evenings sneaking through the trees to be in that place with him, me giddy as a girl even though I was old enough to know better.

Why couldn't I keep quiet, learn to live with how he was? I might have done, if only it hadn't have been her. Rosamond. That's what sent me over, forced me to blurt those words by the bluebells, all my bottled-up anger eating away at me after stumbling on the two of them the previous day. Going at it, like dogs, in what was supposed to be our secret place.

I play the moment over in my head, hoping somehow my actions will be erased. The scene is always identical though; I know it cannot change:

'I'm telling you! You aren't!' I was shouting, staring at him like a lunatic, willing him to react.

'No! You're lying. It's not bloody possible. I know that I am.'

He paced the violet ground like a caged animal, wilder than I'd ever seen him before, his face hardened – the same expression my excuse-for-a-husband wore when he first found out about the two of us.

'Don't tell me what is or isn't anything, John. You're not the only one with secrets.'

He looked deflated, not like him at all, and just stood there for a minute. Finally, he spoke, so quiet I could hardly hear: 'You sure? You know what this means.' Before storming blindly through the trees.

I tried to call after him, because I didn't mean things to go that way but, even though the words were there in my head, all that came out was his name. In any case, I knew nothing I could say would make a difference. Nothing would have unmade the lie. For I'm certain it was. Because how could something so good stem from so much bitterness and hate?

The creaking of the gate makes me glance up through the window: Freddy Oates with the post – though not much today, by the looks of it. He's shuffling more than usual, bowing his head as he comes up the path, rattling the door rather than dropping whatever he's got through the letterbox.

'War Office, Lily,' he stutters as I come to the door, holding a single brown envelope out to me like it's a ticking bomb.

I've pictured this moment in my nightmares, but in them the birds were never singing so sweetly, such a warm breeze was never blowing, and Freddy Oates' simple face was never staring at me so blankly.

I take the letter without reply and pull the door to, shutting myself off from the outside world because it can't be good: nice news doesn't come in brown envelopes. Then again, it can't be something too awful because then surely I would have already had a telegram, wouldn't I? Perhaps they are sending him home on leave, or posting him somewhere safe, away from all the fighting. Maybe, he's got ill or is needed elsewhere. Freddy waits on the doorstep wearing a bewildered expression. Now he's heading back up the path and I can hear him talking to Betty next door. She'll come knocking in a minute, to find out what's what. This village loves a tragedy more than anything else – loves to wallow in someone else's misfortune like pigs in you-know-what. I have to stay strong, mustn't go to pieces for Tom's sake, so focus on the clock, which is still there ticking away above the fireplace.

Ticking away.

I fetch a knife from the drawer and slouch over the table, slicing across the top of the envelope and snatching out the single thin sheet contained within. My eyes scan the typed words and shaky handwriting where some desk clerk has inserted my boy's name:

MORLEY, Thomas
SIR OR MADAM, I regret to inform you...

My mind spins off again, my hand wobbling so much I have to place the paper down before I can read on any further.

Posted as 'missing' on the 15th May 1940.

This does NOT NECESSARILY mean he has been killed, as he may be a prisoner of war, or temporarily separated from his regiment. Official reports that men are being held prisoner take time to reach this country. If the enemy has captured him then, in all probability, unofficial news will reach you first. In such circumstances I ask you to forward any correspondence received to this Office and it will be returned to you as soon as possible.

NOT NECESSARILY.

They wouldn't say that if they really thought he was gone, would they? Surely they're not in the business of dishing out false hope? No, I'm almost positive he's all right. With all the chaos and fighting he must have been taken prisoner. That's what has happened. They'll be holding him somewhere in Germany, but their soldiers will respect the laws and treat him right – they are civilised people. This might even be a mistake – a letter not meant for me – because why didn't I get the telegram when the army first found out? Isn't that what's supposed to happen?

Now a knocking on the door and Betty's excited, questioning voice. Grabbing the letter, I stuff it into my handbag before hurrying out the back through the gardens. I come up further along the lane, passing the wall in front of the farm and the Marshams' house. Their washing can wait, I have to share this with someone who can understand.

Running purposefully, the breeze still blowing and the birds still singing, I cross the grass and hammer their door. She opens it wearing her dark-blue uniform and white pinny from the Hall.

Her eyes grow wide when she sees me, before I've even time to speak.

'Not necessary,' I say, unable to get the words out right.

'What's not necessary?'

'Killed.' Now her face shatters and she drops to the ground, before I can even try to explain. I notice her arm all bloodied and scratched as I slump next to her, trying to keep control of my shivering body. She starts gripping and pulling at her hair with her slender fingers, staring open-mouthed off into space when Kate emerges through the open door.

'What's happened, Mrs Morley?'

'He's missing.'

'Tom?' she says, and I nod. For a moment, I think she will crumple before me too, but she steadies herself and kneels calmly down beside her sister.

'Rachel, do you hear? He's only missing.' Rachel's expression remains blank, fixed straight ahead. 'What's it mean, Mrs Morley – they think he's been captured?'

I nod and now William wanders outside. Such a beautiful boy. So like him. So like his father.

'He may be a prisoner of war,' I say wearily, shaking the letter out of my bag. It falls onto the path beside William, along with John's photograph which has somehow become entwined with the letter. He gives me a sly glance and pockets the picture, passing the sheet of paper to Rachel who stares at the black writing, looking as if she's about to faint again, like she did yesterday. I'm too spent to care what William might make of me having his father's photograph.

'Not necessarily killed,' I say, as Kate helps us both to our feet, guiding us stumbling inside.

WILLIAM

The Germans have taken Tom prisoner, but he will not be afraid. He has bucketfuls of courage – is so much braver than the idiot Air Man – when he worked at the farm he was never scared of cattle: once he even went right in with a bull to stop it getting too frisky.

Rachel, Kate and Mrs Morley sag around the table, gulping tea in silence. Mother has not emerged from her room despite all the commotion. I gather together my school things in the corner. I am taking back *Great Expectations*, which I have finally finished reading, even though it is heavy and fat. In the end of the book it shows you need to be quick and watchful when making a getaway, because if they had rowed a bit faster they would have got Magwitch onto the boat, instead of him getting caught up and fighting with his rival. I am writing a page for Miss Hexham about it which explains how you should not try and be different to what you really are, because the truth will come for you in the end.

Mrs Morley does not sound properly awake. 'I could tell something was wrong when I saw Freddy walk up,' she drones.

'But it's much better news than it might have been, Mrs Morley,' Kate says. 'We don't know anything for certain, so we should look on the bright side – shouldn't we, Rachel?'

Rachel does not respond; her face is filled with blankness. The lines that were on her arm when I came back last night are red and scabbed over this morning. I do not know how she got them, can only think the old tomcat who comes round the house now and then clawed her when she tried to pick him up: a big black thing with cloud-white whiskers and a patch under his chin. Sometimes I see him crossing the field stalking birds, and once watched him devour a whole leveret in one go. He does not like to be picked up – he dug his kicking-feet into me the one time I tried – though you can stroke the top of his head with a finger if you're alert and he's not in a dirty mood.

'Expect we'll hear any day from Tom that he's fine and raring for home,' Kate continues.

Mrs Morley mumbles in agreement and the kitchen goes back to nothing-quiet.

Now I realise: I must have been the last person in this room – in the whole village even – to see Tom the morning he left. I went the long way round to school, through the old orchard. I was hoping to see the little black-and-white woodpecker, because there was a nest in there before and I reckoned there might be one again – only they are secretive, no bigger than a sparrow, and not easy to spot once the leaves have come. I walked slowly through the patchwork of shadows, listening out intently, but could not hear one piping or rattling away, just one of the bigger ones, which flew up in front of me, flashing its flame underside.

I was about at the road when I saw Tom. Hey you, I almost called, but instead thought it would be good to take cover among the trunks and surprise him. As he trudged towards me, a bulging pack of stuff sloped over his shoulder, I kept hidden, ready to jump out. But even though the branches got in my way I could see the way he looked – his face all blackened and one of his eyes closed-up like someone had done a real job on him – so I stayed low, listening to the dull smack of his fading footsteps on the road's hard surface.

Later that evening as him and me burned rubbish in the garden I told what I had seen and asked whether he thought it was the unknown soldier that had done it to Tom.

'Stop gossiping, and don't go upsetting your sister by saying nothing,' he barked, sparks from the bonfire spiralling against the sky like orange-lit glow-worms as he clipped me round the side of the head.

'Get a move on, Billy. You don't want to be late for school!'

Kate is calling over, but I do not care if I am and Miss Hexham will not mind. Besides, why are they going on so? They will never get to the Hall on time themselves if they do not hurry up. Finally Rachel sighs to her feet.

'We ought to go.' Though she does not appear at all ready to me.

'You shouldn't today, not after this shock,' Mrs Morley says and Kate nods in agreement.

'Don't worry, Rachel. I'll explain to Mrs Fisk that you're in no fit state.'

'I'm fine.' She's putting on her shoes, gazing absently about the room.

I lace up my boots and swing my satchel over my shoulder.

'Wait a minute – I must tell Mother what's happened.' Kate runs past me and up the stairs while Mrs Morley goes to the sink and starts washing the cups. 'It'll be alright,' she says to Rachel, but my sister is not listening. Kate comes back down, shaking her head and muttering to herself. Now she prods me towards the door and we all shuffle about outside where Mrs Morley hugs Rachel, who stands hunched like a petrified hare. She goes across and does the same to Kate and, before I can get away, she grabs me too, repeating again, 'Don't you worry, he'll be alright.' She starts along the lane, Kate shouting after her, telling her to let us know the minute she has any news.

'Get going, Billy,' Kate says and I head off in the same direction as Mrs Morley, trying to work out what she was doing with the photograph of him in her bag. Kate and Rachel go into the shed – I hope they are careful not to knock anything over because that would spell disaster for my collection. Fortunately, I cannot catch any sounds to make me anxious and they emerge wheeling their pushbikes across the grass. Rachel mounts awkwardly; I watch from the hedge as my big sister wobbles up the drove, seeming now so small. In front of me Mrs Morley turns into the farmyard – she'll be going round to the back door, because she does the cleaning in the Marshams' house. Now things start to make sense: I remember coming back with him from the Black Sheds one Sunday, him telling me to be wary of women because they sometimes can be witches.

'Are they scary?' I say.

He laughs as we move across the meadow. The fishing has been quiet – two tiny zebra-striped perch and nothing else.

'Can be! Don't do anything to get the wrong side of them or you won't ever hear the end of it till they've got their own back.'

'Have you seen one?'

He looks puzzled, pausing a few seconds before he replies with a big smirk.

'You mean a real witch? My uncle once showed me an old, stoppered green bottle that he reckoned had one inside. He'd threaten to uncork it and let her out if I misbehaved. More likely held some other sort of spirit, knowing him.'

Further along, past the boggy bit all churned up by the cattle's hooves, he starts laughing to himself.

'Dare say I've had a few curses put on me in my time, though.'

This could be why Mrs Morley had his picture! She is a witch and needed it to lay a curse on him – it would explain why everything has turned out this way. I think back to the two of them together in the bluebell wood. She seemed very upset with him and could have been out for revenge – which is why she was shouting out his name. I pull the photograph from my pocket: in it he is as I remember, I think, even though each day is a longer time since I saw him last, and it gets harder to picture him as an actual person and not just someone from before. Someone gone for good.

Now I realise something staring me right in the face: she must have been talking so cross in the woods because of Tom. She was upset over her son joining the army and blamed our family for his going away. She had been storing it up for months and finally took the chance to get her revenge. I think through how it must have happened: to start with, I know that Rachel and Tom were sweet on each other from before, because I watched them kissing once in his old house. When Tom found out she was expecting by another man he would have been furious and persuaded Rachel to tell him who the unknown soldier was so he could confront him. Only, when he did, the soldier must have beat Tom so bad that he had no choice but to go away, which is when I watched him leaving with his pack, his eye all black and puffed. Mrs Morley knew this, which is why she was crying by the bluebells – she expected that he would help Tom sort out the unknown soldier, and be able to persuade him not to go off and join the army, but instead keep working at the farm. Tom would have listened to him, I am sure. And in time Tom and Rachel might even have become sweethearts again, once Tom had forgiven her for being those words.

This must be why Mrs Morley was so upset – why she wanted to curse him – she thought he should have done more to make things right for Tom after Rachel had let her son down like that. But she was not being fair: how would he know which soldier to get even with if Rachel would not tell him? Just because Tom got it out of her somehow does not mean anyone else could

have. I was there when he banged on the table till the plates flew –
I know how stubborn my sister can be.

I turn left onto the main road, the school peering above the
hedge ahead. I pause and look at his photograph again and the
stupidity of the whole idea hits me, because Mrs Morley has
always been nice and does not bother us like so many of the
others. In any case, witches do not exist any more, except in
stories, and if she was really one she would surely just have cast
a spell to prevent Tom from leaving, or to stop him being captured. Not gone around putting a curse on the man who had
always tried to look out for her and her son ever since she became a widow – because he was always popping over to their
house to help her with little odd jobs and things.

Most likely Mrs Morley found the photograph lying about
somewhere; Mother is so forgetful and could easily have
dropped it in church. When Mrs Morley was helping to clean up
in there she probably came across it, putting it in that handbag
she is always carrying, to give back later.

The school bell has started up so I get a move on. At least I
have worked out why the two of them were arguing in the
woods: I am sure it must have been that Mrs Morley was mad at
him for not sorting out the soldier who did that to Rachel, and
who shrank Tom's eye to a slit. Because if he had found that
man first then Tom would not have got beaten up, but stayed
working at the farm.

And today Tom would not be captured or killed.

So, that is what I must do if I catch the Air Man trying to put
it in Kate. Not hang about, but get on quick with what needs to
be done. Because even though nothing can go back like before, I
must still try my best to keep us Abreharts together.

I will be doubly vigilant in future; I do not want to be another
Pip in *Great Expectations*, failing to spot the arch-enemy sneaking up until it is too late. Kate needs to stay here with me,
Rachel and Mother – she must not become like Estella at the end
of the book, sad and broken because she has ended up living her
life with a scoundrel.

We must not all come apart – I will not let us. Because I
promised him. Promised him that I would be the man.

114

RACHEL

The monotony of the back and forth dulls the pain above my eyes; I polish harder at the floorboards, concentrating on the shine to try and banish the visions of Tom that are pushing their way into my head, focussing on a rough spot until my sight becomes blurred. This stops me picturing him, but only for a few seconds, before he appears again, stiff and open-mouthed in a roadside ditch, his green uniform ruptured by bullet holes. Other men are piled behind him in a pathway of bodies stretching to the horizon, but I care nothing about them. Only him.

Kate curves down the stairs, sheets heaped to her chin. She stops and asks in a low voice, 'You holding up?'

I just look at her – I am empty on the inside, no weight remains for me to hold onto. No anything any more.

'Not long now. We'll go for a drink tonight to help take your mind off it, if you want. He'll be alright Rachel. You know what Tom's like.'

I drop again, sliding across the smoothness of the floor. She's off to stuff the sheets into the machine's huge drum, cramming it full and grating the mottled soap on top before flinging in a handful of soda. I want to follow and crawl in beneath them. Get her to fasten down the lid and let the water wash over me, let the machine suck me under.

Instead she's away, and I focus on the back and forth, not caring about the rawness of my knees or the hissing in my head as I scrub round and round. Tom's face comes again, closer now, so his bloodied teeth show. A fly crawls over his peeling lips. I rub the boards more vigorously to rid myself of the apparition, concentrating on the lines I made along my arm last night. They should hurt – I want them to hurt – but I feel nothing. Did I cause Tom to be lost by messing with the needle? I didn't, did I? Surely it was fate or bad luck, a result of Father's interference. If there was a knife within reach I'd take the blade and slice even deeper beneath my whiteness, slitting my insides to let the pure air in.

To make me feel something.

The Colonel shuffles by, through to the sitting room where he has his wireless, not noticing my presence, as usual. Ordinarily his indifference riles me, but today I don't care, am happy to hide behind my insignificance. As he fiddles with the tuning to make the war-talk appear, the crackling in my head joins the static. The noise booms into the hallway – a result of his deafness – and every time a voice emerges he loses it by turning the dial too far; finally he stops, thinking he has found the Home Service, but I can tell it isn't. I concentrate on the floor's shine, trying not to listen to Lord Haw-Haw's nasal whine going on about the fall of Boulogne, because now they are more than far-flung words that do not affect me and I realise I have become one of those women that people in the village will mutter about in whispered embarrassment – if I'm not one already.

I sympathise now with what I overheard someone once say – how the unknowing is harder than being sure. I couldn't grasp this before, but now it makes absolute sense. How can I be expected to care about the everyday until I know for sure, one way or another, what has happened?

The Colonel chunters away to himself, as if he believes the man reading out the words can hear what he is saying and converse with him through the air. Now the voice has finished and the sound fades; he must have switched it off. He emerges from the room, sweeping angrily past me like I am dirt on the floor.

I rise from my knees, which will be red circles beneath the black of my stockings, and go into the sitting room. I switch the wireless back on, raising the volume as loud as it will go and turning the dial so a toneless static overwhelms the emptiness.

The noise fills the air like last night's storm, only louder. And it feels better, a little, now the inside of my head matches the ugly sound all around me.

'Kate, come quick. Your sister's had a turn.'

Mrs Fisk punctuates the crackle and the pair of them slip into the space beside me. My arms hang, redundant, against my sides, copying the blankness in my head.

'She won't move!' says Mrs Fisk, turning off the wireless. 'Sort her out before the Colonel sees.' The fizzing fades to nothing and the room goes silent except for my sister's soft-talking voice.

'Come on, Rachel, let's get you home.' She leads me by the arm. 'Is it alright?' she asks Mrs Fisk.

'Yes girl, get her away. She's no good to anyone like this.'

I follow dumbly, somehow, to where our bikes are leaning, but there's no way I have the balance to mount mine and Kate must realise, because she takes one look before continuing up the drive on foot.

We move in silence. My face is a mask I will wear till I know what has happened; there is no point in smiling or crying or screaming until I am certain.

'Don't worry. Tom'll be fine,' she says.

But she doesn't know, so why bother saying? Would she want me to pretend if her David's aeroplane went down – we're losing so many of them it wouldn't surprise me at all. It's all right, Kate, he's at the bottom of the ocean but will soon float up and drag his fish-eaten carcass cross the fields to be back with you. I picture it now, vivid, almost as if it's already happened – this airman I hardly know, sheer terror on his face, hurtling in a hollow shell towards a fiery sea.

Midway home, the road quiet except for the hypnotic lull of the half-hearted breeze, a thought comes to me which I have to share:

'One thing's worse, Kate. Do you want me to tell you?'

'What do you mean? I don't follow.'

'Worse than unknowing.'

'Rachel stop it. Don't upset yourself.'

'Not having anything of Tom's to remember him by. That's worse. Did you know I threw his bracelet away – and he's never once written me a letter since he left.'

Angry after he went off, I took the bracelet he'd bought and hurled it into the clear cold of the watercress beds, not wanting a single gift or thing of his to ever press against my skin again. That thought didn't last long, though, and later I spent hours sifting my fingers and toes through the stream's soft bed, turning up nothing but stones and weeds.

Kate looks at me funny and I watch her mouth prising itself open. Her lips wobble but nothing comes out.

'What is it?' I ask.

'Doesn't matter.' But I can tell it does, because I know my sister far too well. And she realises too because I can see it in her eyes, wanting to get out.

'What Kate? Tell me.'

117

'No, it's nothing.'

I come to a halt, fixing my eyes hard on hers. I'm all air, rustling leaves and broken sunshine as I wait for more words to flow from her lips. Because now she is about to start she must not stop.

'Tell me,' I say.

'Oh, Rachel. He did, though.' Her voice comes calmly, like another person inside her is doing the talking. 'He wrote you before he went.'

I pull away from her, making myself tall in the middle of the road.

'Tom wrote me a letter?'

'Yes.'

'Where is it?'

'I tore it up. I had to.'

'Why?'

'Because he was ending it with you and I didn't want you to be miserable.'

'Oh Kate! You probably misread it. We'll find the pieces and put it back together.'

I grab her hand and start dragging her by the hand, even though I don't know where it is we should be heading.

'Stop Rachel,' she says, 'it's gone.'

'What were you doing with my letter anyway?'

'He told me to give it to you.'

'So why didn't you?'

Everything about me is fury; I am the opposite of the grey statue which stood less than an hour ago at the Hall, sombre, surrounded by static.

'I didn't want you to read it.'

'What did he say?' I am shouting like a madwoman. 'Tell me what he said!'

I have never felt this way before, like an uncontrollable storm, and I am afraid of what I could do, such is the rage and violence bundled up inside me. Kate shrinks into a terrified, hound-cornered deer, too shocked to do anything except tell me the truth.

'I was late for work, Rachel. In the wrong place at the wrong time. I passed him on my bike halfway to the Hall. He'd his pack slung over his shoulder.'

She starts telling me what happened and my anger subsides, changing into something else as I look through her frightened eyes. Her half-crying doesn't matter because the words Tom said to her come clear as anything and it's like I am the one there, not her.

'Where you off to?'

Tom fixes straight ahead, not turning one little bit to look at Kate when she speaks.

'You're in a good mood today! Aren't you even going to say hello?'

He moves into the sunlight and then she can see: the right half of his face is swollen, a puff of skin obscuring his eye: purple-black and awful.

'Tom, what on earth you done? Does it hurt?'

He doesn't answer, just keeps on, wincing as he swings the dead weight of his pack across to the other shoulder.

'He did it, didn't he?' Kate pedals faster, angling across in front of him so he has to stop. 'I know what's happened. Wasn't a soldier that got Rachel in trouble was it? I knew all along.'

Tom says nothing, just keeps struggling on.

'Looks like he worked it out and caught up with you then?'

Now he stops and turns.

'What do you reckon?'

'Sorry, silly question. Still not told me, though – where you going?'

'Anywhere but here.'

'Well, that's a good plan! What about the farm?'

'I can hardly keep on after what's happened. Not with him there, can I?'

'He'll get over it once his temper's passed – he likes you. Always talking about what you've been up to. Tom this and Tom that. Once he's calmed down he'll come round and you pair can get married. We'll be brother and sister, and I'll be an auntie!'

He starts laughing, then stumbles and drops his bag onto the track and rubs his aching ribs. Kate gets off her bike and helps him over to the verge, flattening some keck with her foot and making a place for them both to sit.

'Not that funny is it, the thought of being stuck with me as your sister-in-law?'

He is snorting even harder now.

'You can tell me if you like?'

'Don't think you need to hear.'

Silence, apart from a lark trilling overhead. He chokes out an occasional pained cough as he stares at his feet.

'Tom! I'm already late for the Hall. I'll get wrong when I arrive. Please tell me! Then go home and get some rest. You shouldn't be wandering the countryside when you can barely walk.'

Now he turns and looks her straight in the face, his dark eyes burning right into her head.

'You really want to know?'

'Yes.'

'You sure? You'll not like it.'

'Don't be silly, Tom. What is it?'

'Alright then, I'll tell you. Makes no difference. Can't stay around here no more anyway.'

'You're scaring me.'

His eyes fix on hers and he speaks, slow and deliberate.

'What you said about me going to be your brother – I am.'

There is silence as she takes in his words. Then she speaks, angry yet excited:

'You two have got married? How could Rachel do that? She knows I've always wanted to be a bridesmaid! This is typical of her, sneaking off and tying the knot in secret like someone out of a book. When?'

He shakes his head.

'We haven't got married. Can't.'

'What you on about? You just said…'

'Kate, I'm already your brother. Always have been. Well, half-brother I suppose.'

His bruised face glares at her like a testament of truth and, even though she doesn't want to, she believes him, can tell he isn't having her on.

And I know from the way she is describing things that this is really how it happened.

'Him and your mother?'

'Yes.'

'No, you've got it wrong. What made you come up with a story like this?'

'He told me last night. I finally plucked up courage to ask his permission for me and Rachel – thought I'd get him in a good mood on his way back from the pub – but he ordered me never to see her again. I said no chance and he started laying into me. He's so bloody strong I couldn't keep him off.'

'Oh Tom.'

'He kept whacking me and I was on the ground with everything spinning. He was shouting and though I thought I'd black out I kept telling him we'd get married anyway, with or without his blessing. That's when he pulled me up – lifted me off the ground – and told me we couldn't. Because of this.'

'He was just trying to stop you and Rachel seeing each other. That's all. He's like that – likes saying stupid hurtful things to get his own way. He was angry about the baby. Let's get you back – your mother will tell you it's a lie.'

'She won't. I asked her when I got home after. Said all of it was true.'

'No, I don't believe her. She's making it up because she doesn't want you to marry my sister.'

He hitches the pack again, groaning as he slings it across his bent back.

'I'm joining up. Getting well away from here. I've written a letter – can't face seeing her. Will post it when I'm settled.'

Hunched in the sunlight he gets a queer expression on his face, like he's just had the perfect idea.

'Why don't you give it her, Kate? You can explain if she don't believe me. If she won't trust what you tell her, make her speak to Mother. It's the only way, with how things are.'

He fumbles in his jacket, pulling out a letter. To Rachel Abrehart.

To me.

The address underneath – but no stamp – all in his scruffy big writing. He hands it shakily to Kate. And like a fool she takes it.

'You'd better get off,' he says, 'else the Colonel will have the dogs out after you.' She nods, for once speechless as she rides the rest of the way up the drove, Tom hobbling behind like a condemned man.

I am calm now and back in myself, the flower-laden branches of the hedgerow bobbing up and down in the wind, giving off the vague scent of aniseed and stale flesh.

'Please, Rachel, I'm sorry.'

'Is that everything? Did he say anything else about coming back for me?'

'No. That was all, I promise.'

'Nothing?'

'I left then. Didn't really know what I was doing. When I came through the gates at the start of the drive I got off my bike and went behind the big wall of rhododendrons. I crawled inside and opened the letter, knowing I shouldn't tell you. Ever.'

'But he asked you to give it to me!'

'I knew no good could come of it, and look what's happened. I should never have said. I don't understand why the words came – they just pushed out my throat.'

'What'd you do with it?'

'The letter? Ripped it into pieces when I'd finished reading and buried the bits beneath all the leaves. I don't believe it, Rachel. It can't be true. Tom must have made it up because he didn't want the responsibility. And to get back at Father for hurting him.'

But I believe every single word; I know it's true.

Everything makes sense now, even if I wish that it didn't. Father off till all hours, the comments he'd sometimes make, the things he'd do: like when Kate and me went to his house in the woods after church one Sunday to try and hear the listeners from Mother's favourite poem. All of a sudden he came stomping out one of the top rooms – not wearing a shirt, his thick chest hairs black like a monkey's – as we giggled our way up the stairs. 'What you two doing here?' he shouted. 'It's not safe, not with the way the floors are. Get down and wait.' He descended a few minutes later, all dishevelled and flushed. 'It's hot. You caught me having a nap.' I would have only been twelve or so and didn't think too much of it, though something seemed odd even then; if it was so dangerous why was he shirtless and asleep up there in the middle of a Sunday morning?

No, it makes perfect sense. I do not need to ask Mrs Morley when we get back, because I know she will confirm the things Kate's said.

'I'm sorry Rachel. I should've given it you. But I didn't know what to do – didn't want to upset Mother or get in trouble with Father.'

'So it was alright to let me go on not knowing?'

'I didn't know what was best. Please! Don't shoot the messenger.'

She is crying and I should pity her. What choice did she have? Only I can't forgive her because if she had said something I could have gone after Tom and stopped him from making such a mistake. We would've got married and there wouldn't have been a thing Father could have done to stop us – his own lies would have protected us. I could have persuaded him. I could have. I don't care who Tom might really be: it changes nothing about the way I feel. I only care about his letter, which I never received.

The letter Kate un-wrote.

Now my mood has turned from anger into something far, far worse. She had a duty to give his words to me, because then I could have stopped it, and him and me would have been together to look after Laura, who would not have become not.

'Please, I'm so sorry!' she whines. 'Don't shoot the messenger.'

Why should everything always turn out so easy for my sister? Sorrys are not enough to put this right. Why shouldn't she share this nothingness?

Don't shoot the messenger? If I had a gun, I'd aim it straight at her head and pull the trigger. Make her like me.

Shattered and broken and dead inside.

WILLIAM

When you know the branches are swaying in the sun-streaked sky, it is hard stuck watching Miss Hexham scrape chalk across black, dust powdering air as she wipes away words. I cannot see outside into the field any more since Mr Croxton taped cardboard over the glass to stop it piercing us if a bomb falls nearby, but a linnet is wittering away and I picture the scene on the other side – quieter than a week ago when every bird was singing their loudest song; now they are all becoming too busy, beginning to sit on eggs and even looking to fill miniature mouths with food. Somewhere out there is the butcher-bird. I found his larder of beetles and butterflies skewered on a fence last week – there was even a tiny shrew impaled right through its crusted eye on a nearby blackthorn – but have only seen his dark highway man's mask the once this spring, as he sat bubbling for a mate from the top of a bush. I hope he finds one because no lady shrike came last summer – he might even be one of the last of his kind left around the village – and I would love to get his egg for my collection.

My legs are jiffling and my mind cannot concentrate on the sums she has set, so I count the children in the room instead: seventeen in all. Joe Scott is the oldest and will be finishing in a few weeks. Next is me. There are two girls one year younger, but the rest are much smaller including some evacuees from London. I don't mix with any of them hardly nowadays because I prefer being by myself, sometimes just tagging along with Joe when the feeling takes me.

Miss Hexham has finished writing and tells us it is drill time. We take our masks out their boxes every day and do this, which is stupid, because why would the Germans want to drop gas on our school when there are bigger places to bomb? She is not as strict about how we put them on as Mr Croxton; he forgets and thinks he is back in the trenches, barking GAS! GAS! at the top of his voice, although it is always just one of our air planes going over. I cannot be bothered to carry the mask home every day so now hide it in a tin under the hedge and pick it up when I arrive each morning.

The smell makes me feel like being sick as the straps pull over my head. My breathing goes like a pig, my sight blocked so I can only see ahead and hardly anything to the side. Finally Miss Hexham says that's enough and I am relieved to peel away the rubber, sucking in the classroom's stale air, which seems fresh by comparison.

Joe is next to me at the back, drawing a bomber in his exercise book like the one I spotted last night, only he puts zigzag lines to show it firing at a Messerschmitt. Joe knows what all the different ones are called – he goes to the base to watch them taking off and even sometimes rides his pushbike to the army camp over Swaffham way to look at them driving the tanks. Air craft and suchlike do not interest me much, though I did go with him once last year, before the war had started, to get a curlew's egg from the field by the base's fence.

Now he leans across and whispers to me, 'Billy, look at this.' I don't like Billy; Kate calls me that name too, though he never once did: always William with him.

Joe's hands move below the desk and he drops something onto my knee: a photograph showing a lady lying on a bed wearing nothing, her arms folded over her bosoms. Joe grins at me.

'My brother gave it me.'

Joe Scott's brother is in the army. Staring ahead at the blackboard I slip it secretly back to him.

'Soldiers get to do it with all the girls because they are so grateful to be saved from the Jerries they just lie there,' he whispers, and at that moment Miss Hexham calls out.

'What are you two chatting about?' I look down at my desk in case my guilty face gives anything away.

'Nothing Miss,' Joe replies, pocketing the picture, then smirking at me when she turns again. Now he is not even whispering, just mouthing, 'What about that!' as he shuffles another across, this time right on top of my desk. Maggie Thompson is staring round at us and shoots her hand up, calling out to Miss Hexham as I fumble the photograph into my pocket.

'What is it, Maggie?'

'Joe Scott and Billy Abrehart are looking at pictures, Miss.'

'Don't be a tell-tale,' she says, coming over and standing right before us. 'Joe, what are you up to?'

'Showing Billy a photograph of my brother in the army, Miss.'

'Well get on with those sums and save it till after school.'

I ignore Joe's smirking face and stare at the clock's hands, willing them to move faster so I can get out the room. Two o'clock. Not long now.

The cock linnet still jangles away. His front is like a robin's, only more pink than orange. Standing at the back of the playground I watch him dive into the hawthorn with a beakful of something – caterpillars, I suppose. I dashed out the classroom when Miss Hexham said it was time and hid before Joe could catch up, mad at him for nearly getting me in trouble. I will be pleased when he stops coming to school, as nobody else here bothers speaking to me much since I stopped answering back, which suits me fine. Besides, they are scared of the time last year when I had the fight with Gerald Fisk. He should not have said those lies, so I kept hitting him, even though he was crying out at me to stop and blood smeared his mouth. He works at the Hall now, but knows better than to say anything about him to me again. He caught me first with one in my stomach, but I ignored the sick feeling and concentrated on the stupid face that spoke them things. Even though he was bigger I surprised him, keeping on punching and kicking till he fell. Then I knelt my knees across the tops of his arms and hit left and right into his lying gob, again and again until Mr Croxton came raring out and dragged me off, Gerald spitting a tooth onto the grey ground.

Mr Croxton's face was crimson as he clouted me round the head, but I heard Joe telling him and Miss Hexham that Gerald had been teasing me, so they knew he deserved everything he got. I was not allowed in school though for the rest of the week, which was good because the holidays started straight after and all sorts of birds and butterflies were about when I went exploring. When I came back after the summer Mr Croxton took me aside all serious and said he understood about how it must be for me, but he would not tolerate any repeat and I must be on my best behaviour.

That is why I am cross with Joe, though I suppose he is all right because he stood up for me before and he has never had one bad word to say against him, not like Gerald.

126

I take Joe's lady photograph out – this one looks more yellow than the other and she is turned around so you cannot see her bosoms, only her backside. I could keep it or scrunch it up, but I suppose Joe will want the picture returned so stuff it below a loose brick under one of the windows. He can get it tomorrow when I tell him. The gas mask is ready so I walk to the hedge and stash the container in its secret place. I should take the stupid thing home, but the Germans do not scare me and I will not need it in the woods. I do check my pocket though, to see if my identity card is still safe. I must carry that at all times, else there will be hell to pay if a police man ever stops me.

As I head along the lane the churchyard draws me in. His spot is round from the main door, in front of a row of old gravestones so worn you can't even read the names. No one else is visiting, except me and the peaceful wind. Weeds rise over a yard tall because the grass has not been mown for a fortnight or more, but I do not think all the insects flying above would bother him. A ladybird crawls along his cross-stick. When she reaches the top she opens her wings and flicks away to a clump of dandelions.

Would he be sad, I wonder, about Tom being missing? I think back to the winter three years ago, the two of us going through the Seven Acre searching for pieces to carve into walking sticks.

'William, what do you reckon to Tom?'

'Tom Morley? He's alright. Showed me a redpoll's nest the other week.'

'Did he? He's a good lad. Not scared of a hard day's work.'

He has found a gnarly old piece of ash with a kink at the top that will make a sturdy grip. His bone-handled knife trims the end neat, the vicious blade whittling off thin strips of bark as we walk back. Crossing the bridge to the meadow he curses and when I turn he has dropped the stick and is shaking his left hand in the air, blood sopping from a nick in his thumb. He puts it into his mouth and sucks before wrapping his handkerchief tight around, the angry stain blushing the cotton.

'You ought to get out with Tom some more – you must get a bit fed up only having sisters for company.'

'Sometimes,' I say.

'Well I'll have a word. I bet he knows where all the best nests are.' I pick up the stick for him and we walk the rest of the way without speaking, listening instead to the pops of our boots as they squelch through the curdled ground.

Now I am sad Tom is missing: sometimes – before he went away – he did take me about and once we found a snipe's nest tucked away in the boggiest part of the meadow where the water overspills. Then, that one time, I watched him and Rachel kissing as I stood in the wood, but I did not mind because he was my friend – not an idiot like Kate's Air Man.

Hopefully our soldiers will soon rescue Tom from the Germans, when they get to wherever he is being kept. Then at least he can come home and forgive Rachel for expecting and she will not have to be so sorrowful any more.

Stones are crunching; that silly old cow Mrs Heckleton is wandering up the path. She has not seen me so I crouch behind a tall stone – *Isaiah Randall 1843–1885* – peering round the side of it to watch her stop before her husband. If I think back I can picture his thin face and thick spectacles: a shrunken grey-haired man who was often sat outside their house when I was little. He would shout out to Mother as we walked by – always about the weather – until one day he was not there and we did not pass him any more. Mother told me he was poorly and I think he must have died not long after. Now the old bag takes out the flowers from the vase against the stone, emptying the silken water and brown leaves onto the grave beside.

'Must bring you some fresh ones, Harold,' she says, and I grin to myself at how stupid she is to talk to him, because he cannot answer back.

'Terrible thunder last night.' And she goes on to describe the storm, which I suppose he would have found interesting, what with liking the weather so much.

'Well, my love, I must get going.'

Grasping the headstone she rattles herself upwards. Age hangs heavy upon her body: her arms are covered in lilac spots, her hair white and wiry, her fingers twisted into a claw. She hobbles inside the church; once the door creaks shut I walk over and study what is written:

128

Harold Heckleton
born 3rd May 1869
died 19th October 1932
Aged 63 years
Beloved Husband and Father

Even though she is an interfering busybody and an old cow, I am suddenly sorry for her. Perhaps the same missing-feeling gnaws away at her like it does me. Being alongside her husband in their garden, watching up with him at the different-shaped clouds overhead might have made her feel the way I do when me and him go walking through the woods and fields. So I will try not to get so angry with her in future when she pokes her nose into what we are doing, because I did not realise he was a Beloved Father too; I could not say if their children are boys or girls as I have never seen them – they must be quite old, I suppose, and left the village before I remember. Seeing the words carved there makes me feel ashamed that there is nothing like that for him; when I am older and earning enough money at the farm I should buy a proper stone with big letters. But then the dates will be written down and final, and his name will be there for everyone to see, and I do not want them all reading and saying his name when they walk past, because it is not theirs to say.

He is NOT THEIRS to talk about.

All this gets me thinking about Laura and the unknown soldier again. He was her father, but never even once got to see her, which is NOT RIGHT. My eyes moisten as I remember holding her on my knee, making her dolly walk the arm of the chair so that she gave her first smile just for me. And even if that bloody man was to turn up here again right this minute he would not ever be able to gaze upon her little face, because she lies over the far side of the churchyard.

Two more crossed sticks in the ground.

Her box was tiny but it looked a real struggle – like it was anchored with lead – as he carried it with the Reverend, the weight of her body pulling him down because he loved her too, too much.

I am still kneeling, quiet, thinking of Laura, when the church door starts grating; I move out of sight, pressing my back into another lichen-scarred stone, whose letters I cannot make out. Mrs Heckleton emerges, only now accompanied by the Reverend; he is nodding and shaking his head as they come to a standstill above Harold Heckleton.

'In these testing times we must pray and have faith. If the worst has happened, at least she can take comfort in Christ.'

'Well, I hate to think how Lily will go if she does lose him. He's all she has,' she says, and they start shuffling towards the lane.

The pair of them are talking about Tom and his mother. I want to open my mouth and let the loudest words fly out, tell him to get lost and shut his fat vicar face! He does not believe that Tom is being held captive but instead thinks he has been killed in the fighting. With the Germans in their tanks it must have been dangerous and difficult to keep out the way of all those whizzing bullets and grenades, so perhaps they are right. Mr Croxton told us how courageous our men are being, helping the French to grasp victory from the mouth of defeat. But what if a bullet slammed into Tom's head as he waded through the boiling mud of the battlefield? His body would have been tramped way down into the ground so that nobody even realised. And I do not want him to be gone because then I will know of another person lying under the earth:

Already there is him. And Laura. Then my grandparents, who I never met, though Grandfather Sampson was still here when I was a baby, before the horse decided to kick out its hoof. Even others from the village, too, like the boy who suddenly stopped coming to school – they whispered he had been taken by men in something – back when I was very small. So, Tom must not join with them too, else there will be nearly as many down below as up here. And despite what the Reverend says I do not believe a single one has been gloriously transformed, because he does not have any way to prove it. All he can do is preach about faith – about how it must remain strong – but why should I trust his puffed-up face about anything, without a trace of proof?

The Reverend is tricky, though; he tries to make it seem more believable by talking about the soul, which is invisible. It is the thing, he says, which makes us what we are. A soul is like a ghost, only inside a person's body, and I think ghosts might also be what they call lost souls. He explained this to us when he came to school at Easter to teach us of Jesus who, even though they nailed his hands onto the cross so he bled until he died, rose again. And when he became re-alive it was not as an invisible soul, but in his real body, because he showed the holes to Thomas, who had doubted him.

Men, says the Reverend, get to Heaven through the goodness of their souls. Only Jesus was a special case, which I suppose is what you would expect. God would value his son above anything else and want him never to change, and never to die – so when they rolled back the stone his body had got up and walked away. But with normal men it is only the soul that goes up, he says. Yet no one has even seen a soul because they are invisible, which is very convenient for the Reverend and all those others, as it makes their words difficult to disprove. Like when Joe Scott told me a peregrine falcon had just flown above our heads – although we looked about everywhere, afterwards I realised he said it to make me go with him through a part of the woods he was scared of, because he thought the listeners would get him if he went past the house on his own.

I think the Reverend is unsure of the ins and outs of how it all works because some weeks he preaches the body is only ashes and dust, and on other occasions there is also the flesh. It seems to me he makes up the rules as he goes along, changing them to suit whatever he wants to say. But I try and concentrate on the facts, because with something such as this you have to be like a detective in a story to solve the different parts of the puzzle.

So, for what he is saying about the glorious transformation to be true and for Heaven and Hell to exist, I must work out the order in which things would need to happen:

1. Firstly the person dies.
2. They are buried in the ground.
3. The body, or the soul, escapes the coffin and makes its way, somehow, to the surface.
4. The body, or the soul, makes its way from the ground up to Heaven, way up in the sky above the clouds.
5. The body, or the soul, arrives in Heaven, where the final judgement is made. If the person fails the test they are flung back to earth and swept down by the Devil to wherever that other place lies.

6. This is how it could work.

Now, if bodies clawed their way up, like the way you dig for potatoes in the garden, there would be no mystery. Everyone would know what becomes of us because all the opened graves would be unmissable. So that is not a possibility.

And even if a corpse did get to the surface it could not just flap its arms and fly off into the sky; in order to get to Heaven it would need to travel in something, else no one at all would have made it up there before air planes were invented – or at least before hot air balloons. And that means millions of bodies wandering around with nowhere to go, which is clearly not the case.

So if we do get to Heaven, it has to be through our souls, like the Reverend says.

And now I wonder... Looking at the weeds winding about my feet and shins I notice how many molehills burst up in this place – they are not easy to spot with everything growing so tall, which is perhaps why I have not thought this ever before: what if they are the up-tunnels? Not person-sized holes, but smaller – though still big enough, I would think, for a soul to squeeze through.

Perhaps the body changes into a mole for the first part, one of the best animals to be if you need to dig your way out of a place. This might be what the Reverend means with his glorious transformation. Not something that happens up in Heaven, but a way for the soul to arrive there in the first place!

I go over to his bit of ground. Yes! Even here, beneath all the grass, the soil is broken and black where one has burrowed up. Perhaps he did transform, like the Reverend said. Only he would not want to stay a mole for long, because he used to trap them at the farm and string them along the barbed wire against the meadow to warn the others to keep away and stop ruining the pasture.

Once at the surface I suppose the mole might change again to get even higher. Or maybe the soul jumps out of the mole into a creature more suited to getting up to a great height.

Like a bird.

Is it possible? I let my thoughts wheel about inside my head. Thinking about it, I realise the owl appeared in his house for the first time a year to the day that they lowered the ropes. And if he had to transform into anything I know that he would be an owl.

It would make sense because of what he showed me in the barn – and even the shape of his nose, which Kate said was like a beak. In which case, has he come back to live in the house he was born, rather than going up to Heaven? Or, as that is where it happened, has he become a lost soul forced to remain in that place forever?

Not as a man, but as an owl.

As I walk home, my mind races. Hopefully he will show me a sign or something so I can prove whether this new idea is THE TRUTH or just more BLOODY LIES. Mother is stabbing her little trowel into the soil of the front bed as I pass, so intent on what she is doing she does not seem to notice me. The house is quiet as I stand by the door removing my boots. Kate is leaning her head on the table, she must have got home early from the Hall; I cannot see Rachel anywhere. My thirst has got up so I pour a lukewarm glass of water from the jug and settle against my sister. She does not speak, but her face wears an anxious expression, all puffy and pale. Perhaps her Air Man is missing, or she too is worried about Tom.

I get out one of my school books and start to draw with a pencil exactly how the owl was sat last night. Only the outline of his wings and face – because he is almost all white it is not possible to colour him in. The eyes are the hardest to get right: though at first they appear like dull black circles, when you look closer they actually shine and catch the moonlight so you can see other shapes and reflections moving within. If he lets me get near enough later, even for one second, I am sure I will be able to make out my own face in there. Just like in a mirror.

The more I think about them the more they seem like his eyes from before. Eyes that have seen everything round here that has ever happened.

'What you drawing, Billy?' Kate asks, making me lose my concentration as I dot the wings and back with little grey splodges. I show her the paper.

'That's nice. Is it a hawk?' I give her a dirty look and keep shading – she could not tell an owl from a hawk if it swooped down and clawed off her face.

Now Rachel steals inside and Kate shoots up from her chair. I carry on drawing, adding in the rafter his talons gripped, the empty window, and even the fat moon outside. Later I may put in

133

the woodcock or the bomber, though they might spoil it because I know now that the owl is the most important.

'Rachel...' Kate half-shouts, but Rachel ignores her, pushing past and clomping up the stairs. She must still be crazed about Tom. Perhaps now she has had time to ponder it she thinks the same as the Reverend and Mrs Heckleton – that he took a German bullet as he led a heroic charge and has now sunk down to lie beneath all the mud.

Kate grabs me hard across my wrist, making one of my walls go wonky. This angers me and I snatch back my hand.

'Listen Billy, Rachel's upset.' She looks serious, squinting right into my face. 'I need to go to Summer End later, so I want you to watch her. Make sure she don't do nothing silly.'

Kate's cheeks are red and blushing, as if she has been crying.

'Will you do that?'

I nod, though really I should follow her, because I am certain she must be meeting the Air Man and this is a trick to get me off their scent. But I do not mind too much because the weather is holding fair and it will be a good time to see him again: I need to find proof one way or the other.

'Thanks, you're not a bad little brother sometimes,' and she pats me on the head like I am a drooling baby.

Rachel did not come down for tea – jam sandwiches that Kate made. She took them upstairs but Rachel would not open the door so her plate rests on the floor outside their room. Kate is fussing around because I think she wanted to wear a different dress, only she cannot get inside to put one on.

Sleepiness washes over me after coming back so late last night. I must be wide awake when I go out again, so I lie down on my bed. My eyelids start to relax, it will not take long. My mind is already imagining his creamy, rounded wings shimmering in the moonlight as he alights upon his perching place.

'Well, William,' he will whistle through his hooked beak. 'You have worked it all out. And now I am back for ever.'

RACHEL

If I will it hard enough, can I turn the thing my sister told me to a lie? Can I force the truth away? Why, Kate, could you not have waited for Tom to return – at least then I'd be able to ask him to his face, to see if he feels a difference? Because it doesn't matter to me. Doesn't change the thing we were together – the way we still should be – one little bit.

I mean this. All of it. Until my head conjures up the image of my father rearing out the ground, his eyes like Tom's, only with a ferocity inside them that makes me flinch. And I wonder, however much I fight it, if things can ever be quite the same now I possess this dirty knowledge. Even though I want, so much, to stop myself from caring.

Mother and William are both sleeping, I think, despite the early hour. Kate has gone off; I saw her through the window, cycling up the drove. I can't speak to her any more, she should not have done what she did. We are sisters but that means nothing now. She should have delivered Tom's note, even if she couldn't bear to tell me his news with her own lips. His words shouldn't have been buried like that.

I will not be an ignorant girl stumbling blind in the shadows.

No, Kate is to blame for not doing what was right. For not telling me the truth, and for letting me harbour wrong thoughts of Tom when he went away. Because he supposed he had no choice, even though he was mistaken and it didn't matter: Laura was still the same little girl she was when we did the thing that made her – she was still perfect – and no one can ever tell me my daughter was created out of sin. Because we did not know. And what was between us was so pure.

Kate's guilt is nothing compared to Mrs Morley, though. She's the whore, not me. Always coming round here helping us after Father had gone, only not out of kindness to Mother, like I thought, but a way of easing the guilt which must eat at her insides.

Then there is him.

How could he call me those things after betraying Mother all that time? How could he say anything bad to me, let alone expect

Tom and me to suffer for his mistakes? He should've accepted the consequences of his actions, kept his mouth shut and his fists at his sides, rather than sending Tom away in secret. Afterwards acting the innocent, all sweetness round Laura, so before long I started to believe he wasn't to blame for breaking us apart. Though now I know it was all down to him. And I hope he burns in Hell. I should go to where he lies and do to him like he did to me. My father might have believed himself something special, because he was top of the muckheap at the farm – Lord of the Harvest and all the rest of it, the village worshipping the ground he trod on – but he was less than a man to spit in my face when my beautiful baby was growing inside my belly.

I'll wake Mother and tell her everything; she deserves the truth and I shouldn't be like Kate, too afraid to speak. How she'll take it, so flimsy anyhow these days, I don't know. Will learning, after all this time, that the husband she loved was dirt, be of any comfort? I hesitate. Perhaps it's best to keep quiet, to let her remain in innocence like William, with her daydreams and daffodils. But I can't ever forgive Mrs Morley or Father. And Kate can handle her own petty worries from here on in – I won't help her again after she's betrayed me like this.

Only Tom can I excuse. Because however weak he was to go away – not even coming back to see Laura off – and however the world might judge the two of us together, I cannot stop myself from wanting him.

I lie drowsy and drained. The bedroom is muggy and it's hard to breathe. Like being trapped inside something; like the story Father told me, which he said happened at the Hall years ago, though I'm sure it was just another of his endless fairy tales.

Another of his lies.

In the story a beautiful girl has married the young Lord. After the ceremony as part of the celebrations, the guests play hide and seek, his Lordship having to look for them all. The new bride scampers to the top of the house where, in the back of one of the little-used rooms behind lots of junk and covered-over furniture, she comes across a wooden chest. She goes to open it, thinking it'll be heavy, but it's light as the sky so she climbs inside and closes the lid. In the rest of the rooms the game continues, her husband gradually uncovering the hiding places of the other guests, until she is the last to remain uncaught. After an hour there's no sign and he's ready to admit defeat. He stands laughing on the grand staircase, shouting at her to come out, telling her she has won and to come claim her prize. Only she doesn't appear and soon they are all worried, scouring the Hall and its grounds for hours. Nothing. Days later still he is searching – along with all the servants and people from the nearby villages – but to no avail.

The girl has vanished.

He becomes a broken man, unable to sleep, going out of his mind, prowling the house and barking at the staff. Wondering if he said or did something to drive her away? Whether she found out something about him that made her change her mind?

A year later, on one of his dazed rambles, he comes upon the unremembered room with the chest. It will not budge so he calls for his strongest servant. Together the pair of them finally pry open the weighty lid. Inside, pale and perfect like she's sleeping, is his bride: perfectly preserved, untouched by time, though not by death. Once nestled within the thick coffin she could not get out – her silent cries for help, which helped to extinguish the last of the chest's air, going unheard.

Like me. Choking in this house, waiting for Tom to release me.

A knocking. At first I ignore it – not one person in the village I can face talking to – but its incessant beat keeps hammering and a man's voice is calling out.

'Anybody there?'

If I leave it, Mother or William will wake and I don't want to see them either, so I go down and through the kitchen, pressing on the handle of the front door. It's her stuttering airman, standing on the step; he seems perplexed.

'Didn't think anyone was in. Is your sister here?'

'No.'

'Know where she's gone? I need to see her.'

'Out.' I struggle to eject the word, because I feel faint here in the doorway, in view of so much air and sky.

'You alright?' he asks, and the thoughts are spinning around my head so fast I'm not sure if I'm able to stay on my feet. My

137

eyes start to stream and there's nothing I can do to stop myself except cover my face with my hand. But the tears slide anyway. He passes me a handkerchief from his pocket, which I gratefully snatch. I dab at my eyes and pass it back to him.

'Hang on to it,' he says. 'I'm a good listener if you want someone to talk to.'

'You can't help.'

'Try me, if you like. I've a good supply of hankies.'

He chats away trying to be nice, but I'm not in the mood, just want to sit in silence in the kitchen's grey light. I should close the door on him, but for some reason when he asks why I'm upset I tell him.

'My Tom. He's missing, they think.'

'I'm sure he'll be fine,' he says, after a long pause. 'Probably taken prisoner. From what they say the camps aren't so bad – be back before you know it.'

At this my tears restart, only now the floodgates have opened and they're raining down.

'I'm sorry,' I say through my sobs, and he hands over another handkerchief. I pass him the soaked old one and this time he doesn't refuse.

'You and – Tom is it? – you'll both look back at today in years to come and laugh.'

The thought of one day being with him and laughing sets me off again. I cannot stop it, any of it. Cannot make it go back to being like before. I lean against the doorframe for support to prevent myself from falling. He looks embarrassed, doesn't know what he should do.

'Want me to fetch anyone? Your mother or someone?'

I shake my head and try to speak. A whispered 'no' creeps from my mouth.

'Well, if you're sure... Look, I'd better go find your sister – if she turns up tell her I came.'

He is trudging across the grass when it strikes me: how I can punish Kate.

I know he will do it, because he has that look set onto his face. And I don't care any more because nothing good is left within me, so why not? Let her feel it too, because she is right and there might as well be no consequences to the things we do.

138

'Wait! I need some air. Won't you walk with me?'

I set off after him, the pressing-down squeezing behind my eyes like when a head cold fills your sinuses. No time for talk because I am readying myself: I will make Kate share the feeling. Then the sky can come down and replace the badness lurking inside, the bad luck that makes these things happen. Like when I was sticking the needle last night and my blood flowed out. Only now, if I let him, he can take it all from within me and empty it away.

I lead him along the path through the trees, past the bluebells and the still-screeching rooks until we are in the openness of the meadow, the tall grass damp against my bare calves: I know what has to be done. I think of going to the house of my father, where Tom and me listened for the voices, but realise the first place will be better.

'Where we going?' he asks, his expression all beguiled and ignorant. I do not reply, just lead him silently on.

At the bridge I wade into the stream, my toes trawling the sandy floor beneath which my lover's rusted bracelet surely lies. I jink effortlessly forward, like a water-spirit, while David dawdles on the bridge, clumsy and foolish as he struggles with his boots.

This is the place. The place me and Tom came that first time.

Pushing through the overhanging branches the interior is not like I remembered: the air inside is cooler and quieter, lacking the insect hum and noisy whirr of the fast-spinning world from before.

'Hang on!'

'In here,' I call, and he scrambles up the bank.

'Water's a bit nippy – I got a right soaking!'

I ask for his jacket; he hands it over, without question, and I lay it on the ground. Now I remove my clothes, quickly and mechanically until everything has gone. My skin is see-though, my hair falls lankly across my face as I lower my body onto the jacket and lie open before him.

He looks dumbstruck.

I stare at him wilfully, daring him down: I have emptied my head and want him to get on and do it so Kate can know too – why should I be the only one to feel this nothing? Because I cannot care about any of it until I'm certain what has happened to Tom. She should know how it is too; she should learn about loss.

Like I have learned.

David unbuttons his shirt and casts it aside, kneeling above me and kissing my stomach, the stubble of his chin brushing against the faint stretch marks Laura left me; I do not want to look at his face, just get on and suffer my due. Perhaps this will remind me of hate, or regret. Something better than empty at least.

Now he has his trousers down and is inside me, pushing and grunting to cover my silence, but still the nothingness persists. I dig my fingernails into his skin to urge him harder, but it does not help because the faster he thrusts the less I feel. Not like with Tom, where everything about the way the world moved had meaning.

I cannot bear to look into his face as he shoves back and forth; he is grinning and thinks this is special, thinks that I care and this means something. I should have some guilt – if not for my sister, then for him – but if he were any better than me he would not be doing this either. I turn my face and concentrate on a dark, chestnut-coloured beetle that is crawling intently along the ground; the trees away and beyond are all greenery and rustling.

Then a shadow, a shape, and a thud: his weight pinning me in a final lunge as his head lolls up at the swaying, shrouding branches.

WILLIAM

Midway between sleep and awareness I remember the look in his eyes: like the gaping whites of a bullock being loaded onto the slaughterhouse lorry. The stare bores through me until I force it to stop and make better thoughts come.

The now-sounds outside – the swifts squealing excitedly back and forth to the eaves – mix with those in my head, and I am in that evening three years ago. As I go past the trees which guard the outline of his old house, I think I can hear a noise inside and wonder if it is the people Rachel told me about. I decide to look even though he said I should never pass below the doorframe's hanging ivy because the crumbling walls could collapse without a moment's warning.

I creep through the thick greenness, along a path someone must have made – an animal would not have come this way and it has been deliberately hacked. The door stands open so I do not have to push it any further to squeeze inside. I pause; the sound seems to have stopped – perhaps nothing more than my imaginings. Against the stairs, I stand tree-still and make my breathing noiseless so I will be able to pick out anything. The place is cold and I do not like waiting here because of what Rachel said about them listening, and what he told me about the house falling down. I am all set to leave when it comes again, high-pitched and clear as a yaffle's laugh: a lady's voice upstairs. I want to be brave and climb to see, but my legs have turned to water and I cannot stop myself shouting out in return, begging them to leave me alone. Then I am blundering back, not daring to turn till I reach the safety of home.

Wheezing and breathless I want to tell him, but he is not there – my sisters will only tease me, and Mother will be all bothered, so I stay quiet. Soon he comes in, realising straight-away I am not right. He takes me outside and we head up the drove.

'Seen something that frightened you, William?' he asks.

'No, I heard it – there was a voice.'

'Where?'

At first I do not want to say, as he has told me so many times before not to go under the ivy because of the dangers. But when he studies my face, I find I cannot lie.

'Your house in the woods. I stood by the door and a lady's laugh came.'

'Did you see or hear anything else?'

'Just the laughing. Rachel said it's a ghost house.'

'You're certain? You didn't see anything?'

As I shake my head I think he will be mad and shout because I went where I shouldn't. Instead he swivels me onto his shoulders for a piggyback – even though I am far too big. But he is so strong it is not a problem.

'Listen, you mustn't ever go there again. Rachel's right and it's bad luck to hear them. Promise me?'

'Yes,' I say.

'Good lad. Now, we shouldn't tell anyone of this. Your mother wouldn't like to think you'd been playing inside because it's dangerous, and your sisters would be frightened.'

I nod and we start heading home.

'I'd have been scared of the voice too, William. So for being so brave and not telling I want you to have this.' He pops me down on the road and gets out his second knife, the smaller one with the brown leather sheath.

'Be careful, it's sharp,' and I grin up at him as he places it in my hands. 'Remember – not a single word.'

Nothing about the world seems changed when I rouse from my remembering. The light in my bedroom remains the same and a constant breeze funnels through the open window. The swifts are still screaming, the other birds tight-beaked. I can hear talking below – the Air Man's stupid voice is floating up from the garden. Through the glass I see the top of his head with its fluffed brown hair. Kate told me she was going out, so why is he here – I thought she would be meeting him in Summer End. Two voices now; I cannot make their actual words out but realise one belongs to Rachel. This is better as it means he will soon be off. He starts pacing across the grass, twiddling his hands behind his back. Just as he gets to the far side Rachel shouts over at him and after a minute she emerges, slamming the door and striding

142

into the trees. He snakes after her, which is wrong, because she should have sent him packing, not go off walking with him. I wanted to concentrate on finding the owl this evening, to see if it really is him; now I will have to follow them first.

Keeping my distance, I become like the old tomcat when he stalks his prey in the fields. My feet make no noise and my jacket blends against the nettles and leaves. I keep the pair of them at the edge of my sight, waiting by the gate until they get to the line of trees that straddles the meadow's centre. Once they have disappeared beneath its dark dividing line, I move into the open, still concentrating on their movements through the trunks. I reach the bare earth of the break – the floor stripped of all vegetation where the cattle roll and rest up during hot days and when the rain is falling hard – without being spotted. They are nearly to the fence now, Rachel a long way in front, him following like an obedient dog. She mounts the stile to the watercress beds and now I cannot see her, just him bounding behind. I wait among the halfway trees and bushes, because if they are on the bridge they will surely notice me as I cross the rest of the meadow's emptiness.

Above my head hangs a mossy ball bound together with spider's thread, like some tiny seamstress has been busy with a needle: a long-tailed tit's nest. I place a finger through the entrance hole and feel the soft lining of feathers inside: paper-dry to touch, I can tell it is last year's – if it were fresh there would be a whole load of eggs cushioned within, at least eight and maybe more, glossy white with red speckles. I wonder how many of the fluffy, pied chicks made it to the wing and into the safety of the woods before the magpies and weasels and crows finished them off.

The wait has been long enough. If I skirt around to the bridge from the side, I should be able to listen – if they are close enough – without them seeing me; if they have pressed further on, I will soon catch them up. I move in a low arc until I reach the fence. No sounds come from the other side of the rushes, but I cannot be sure, so pause again before the stile. He told me once about how the Devil used to sit atop the one back of Summer End churchyard on a certain night of the year, playing his pipe to charm unwary travellers into following him. Because the thick yew hedge makes that spot so shaded, I suppose you would think him only a man, until you were right upon him and it were too late.

In any case, I am not worried as this is a different place and a different stile. I head onto the bridge; the pair of them are nowhere, so I continue across. The plank bows beneath my weight, slapping gently against the water with each step, before I scramble up the steep slope into the wood at the far bank. I do not see any footprints in the soft mud at the top, but they cannot have got far. Leaves swish in the breeze, the branches sway from side to side. Pausing to let my eyes grow accustomed to the dappled light, I can hear the Air Man ahead in the trees.

I try to pinpoint the noise: he is below me somewhere. I proceed quiet as I can, pleased the wind has got up enough to cover the movement-sounds I cannot help but make. His low-pitched murmur comes again, but still I do not see him – he must be by the water; I will have to break off the main path and slink down the slope where the nettles and ferns grow thickest. From there, I should be able to peer underneath the overhanging branches of the big willow.

Each slow step brings a painful sting as the stems reach up their bristles. I do not cry out even though it hurts, because of the importance of what I am doing. Besides, it will be worse later when the tingling really starts. I move furtively – a word Miss Hexham used at school this morning as she caught Joe sneaking a toffee into his mouth – creeping onto the dark moss of the clearing that circles their hiding place. I crouch on my knees and rest my head on the ground. At first it is hard to make out the shapes behind the veil of willow. Only movement.

Working cautiously around, I edge towards a better spot. My eyes line up with a gap and I spy pale flesh within: not one person's body, but two – all twisted like a pair of entwined slow-worms. Slow-worms keep wriggling if you slice them in half with a spade; they never stop moving, even when they are dead, he told me. Shifting further across the view is clearer: the Air Man's arse bobs up and down on top, the under-body staying limp. Rachel's face remains unrevealed, but it must be her lying beneath him with her legs all bent back. His thing goes in and out of the dark nest of hairs that marks his target.

144

He is putting it inside her.

My stomach wants to retch but I stop myself, stuffing my sleeve into my mouth. I move round to get a better angle so I can check whether she is all right: now I see my eldest sister's expression as the Air Man kneads her bosoms in his hands.

Her eyes are open, but they look dull and dead.

CLACK.

My knee snaps a tiny twig and she blinks, her gaze darting in my direction. I shrink back into the nettles: she does not call out, so I do not think she has noticed me. A big stag beetle ambles past my elbow in an unwavering straight line towards where they are lying. Through the green I catch glimpses of the air man's in and out getting quicker as he pushes her legs further and further back. His grunts are becoming half-words and I fumble inside my pocket, hoping I have the knife with me, though already knowing I had no time to bring it from where I keep it by my bed. If it were in my hand I could make him stop, like I promised I would. Stab the point in him just as he is stabbing himself into my sister. My head throbs and I cannot breathe right. Down at my feet, as if placed here ready for this moment, is a length of wrist-thick oak; I pick it up and caress its solid weight.

Without thinking, I burst from the nettles, a sound I did not know I could make flying from the pit of my stomach as the branches divide before me. I am like the breeze, invisible and unstoppable: the trees a part of my arm as I club him, hard, round the back of his Air Man's head. He slumps forward onto her white belly, and I slouch top-heavy away, stingers scratching my face as I race upslope, running and skidding over the bridge. My foot slips on the wet and I am splashing beneath the surface, then vaulting the stile in a shower of droplets, into the vast openness of the meadow beyond.

I have killed the Air Man.

I meant to, I think, but now I am not sure why. Because even though what he was doing was not right, and even though I promised to look after my sisters, I feel dizzy and wrong. Not proud and relieved as I should. No blood flew when the wood whacked his head, but his hard shudder jarred my arm and he dropped like a downed pheasant. Rachel's eyes went from empty

to scared as she watched me blur the branches and knock him
on top of her. I should go back and hide his body under the
leaves, but I cannot bear the sight of his dead face peering up at
me. Not yet.

I rise from where I was curled among the long grass and walk.
The day is fading and the trees guarding his house begin to
gather the light. Along the dark path I go, pushing half-blind
past the hanging creepers and roaring up answerless to where his
pale, slender body should be.

The walls take my words – my first in more than a year – and
spit them back, so it is not me who is asking but this place. The
questions twist, answerless, inside the room, reverberating against
the dank emptiness until I can stand them no more.

'WHY DID YOU? WHY?'

But his perch is empty, just a mess of white shit shotgunned
across the boards below.

146

MOTHER

Dusk's cloying odour drifts through the half-open window, calling me into the colourless grey of evening so that I descend the stairs without questioning where it is I am headed. Outside, in the front garden, I snap off the last of the thin-stemmed tulips, bunching my harvest in a limp bundle before stepping along the hardness of the lane towards the church. Past the round tower and its glistening flints, beyond the unkempt scattering of cowslips and daisies that garland the graves, to the shade of the far corner. I kneel among the lush swathes of clover and let the darkness transport me back to when I first became Not-Louise, unable to control the ill luck which came flooding thick and fast in that long, scarlet night. The night I have tried so hard to wipe from my memory.

'All over. It's all over.' Mrs Beck the midwife kneels beside her, repeating the words with the rhythm of a lullaby.

And the pain and the blood Louise never knew possible has subsided, allowing her shouts to give way to the room's unnatural silence. Only she can tell something is not right from the rigid expressions on their faces.

'What's happening?'

Her mother is holding a damp flannel to her forehead. 'Shush. Just rest, my girl,' she whispers.

Nan has turned away, trying to suppress a wrenching sob that bubbles inexorably from the bottom of her stomach, her mouth gulping like an air-starved fish. But, even though Louise is more tired than she can ever remember, she cannot rest, because Mrs Beck is standing at the foot of the bed, carefully wrapping a white bundle.

'What? What's wrong?'

As she calls out, her mother leans down and clings to her, as if to stop her from sliding away, speaking the words that can never be forgotten:

'She wasn't meant for this world, Louise.'

Although Louise somehow knows this already, she still has to see for herself. She is calm and strong as Mrs Beck passes across her swaddled child, the most perfect creation Louise has ever looked upon: an angel with tiny hands; so small and still. Nan stumbles from the room, but even her wailing outside cannot disturb this precious smoke-in-the-wind time with her baby, whose name is known only to Louise. As she cradles her dead daughter, tears trickle down the creases of her face like rivulets of water flowing along the furrows of a freshly ploughed field.

Mother fetches John, who stands stone-like in the doorway.

'Do you want to hold our little girl?' Louise implores, but he stares wordlessly at his wife of five months, an absent expression in his eyes, before leaving the room. Later, as their tiny firstborn is laid to rest like an unwanted accident in the back corner of the churchyard, he is too busy at the farm to join her; surely, she thinks, the other men must question his not being present to pay his last respects and comfort his wife.

But the girl with the secret name is gone, and they do not talk of her again.

Louise wonders whether people in the village believe mentioning the unmentionable will allow the ill luck to spread its infection. In her own case, she realises, the sadness is too great: if she speaks of her daughter out loud, nothing will be able to hold back the crushing weight of her sorrow. Yet afterwards, for months in the darkness, Louise's fingers feel the smoothness of her baby's cheeks in the leaden air as she searches for sleep against John's dead-to-the-world body. Sometimes his arm encroaches her hip, his calloused hand stroking her skin before she pushes it away.

All the time John says nothing, not even on The Anniversary, when he looks at her like it is any normal day – not one that should be remembered with the utmost reverence and solemnity. In the evening as they lie together, she asks him: 'Do you know what today is?'

'Thursday.'

'It's her birthday.'

There is silence before he replies: 'What do you expect of me, Louise?' And he turns onto his side, soon stiff with slumber, unlike her own restless body, which has to flee into the night, to where the wind makes the branches bow and creak.

To where I kneel now in the corner of the churchyard, slow-drowning in my salty tears.

RACHEL

Dead weight crushes my stomach and, although I try to roll him off, I cannot, because it is more than the immensity of his body that is pinning me. My hands do not want to touch his clammy back, where his sweat has formed a cold film. Nor his sticky hair, nor the angry swelling on his head. As I wonder how to move him there comes a distant voice, familiar yet strange.

William. He is shouting out, mimicking the crazed sounds he made as they placed our father in the earth.

What chain of events have I set in motion by laying here with David? He is still inside me, I realise, although now shrunken – his seed spreading down my thigh like a snail's glistening trail. I cannot wipe it away because of his heaviness, though the thought of what it could become repulses me.

Not something beautiful, like the memory of Laura that I've sullied.

My body aches from the pressing force and I twist my shoulders, finally shoving him onto the ground in a motionless sprawl. I stumble to my feet and push through the branches, which catch like fishhooks, before sliding down the bank. I plunge forward so that I lie flat on my stomach, the yard-deep stream barely covering my nakedness. Twisting in the grey water, I scrub my fingernails against my skin, then wipe away his stickiness and stand shaking in the evening's chill. Back underneath the willow, I dry myself on his jacket, pulling on my underwear and dress, which cling to my wet body.

Clarity returns to my head – the static fizzle of earlier gone – I can think clearly again, my anger with Kate diminished. Now only shame remains at the thing I've done, made a hundred times worse by the sight of David's carcass spreadeagled on the floor. A feeling of panic is growing inside me; I go across to try and wake him, prodding and poking him to be certain. Nothing, as I knew there would be. His vacant eyes stare skywards.

I should find my brother, to stop him from doing anything else tonight that we will all regret. I wade towards the bridge and into the meadow. As I come to where the trees stand thicker, I wonder whether my brother will be inside that hidden, ruined shell, so step swiftly along the crude path. Ducking past the skewed, paint-flaked door, I pause, looking up at the missing steps which caused Father to trip and meet his maker; this very spot must be where he spoke his last, though my brother has never mentioned any of what passed between them that fateful Sunday. The Doctor said he'd fallen and hit his head, causing his heart to stop; Mother's face blanched as he told us.

Silence. No crying children like in my dream. I stare round the room, stripped now of the life Tom and I lent it with our candles and our love, and the life it gave us back in return.

'Is there anybody there?' I shout. I am the Listener. Or perhaps the Traveller, waiting for an answer that never comes.

Nothing, except a faint ticking in the walls; the trees, I think, brushing their branches against the crumbling stonework. I hope William has fled home and is all right. Perhaps he will finally talk to me – his story needs to square with mine if I am to protect him from what has happened tonight. Only first, I must deal with David.

Outside, the air is choked with nettle-scent; I do not look back at the house's sorry husk as I weave into the faded field, empty of cattle and any other signs of life except a white owl, which is skimming above the tall grass, its lazy flight parallel to the fence. Its eyes concentrate on the ground so it does not notice my presence until almost upon me, swerving silently into the wood at the last moment.

The stream is black now, reflecting the darkness of the clouds piling up above. As I climb the bank I wonder, for a second, whether he will be upright and alert when I push through the curtain of willow. But he's still angled across the ground in the same position I left him. This is no proper place to hide a body – the smell won't take long to attract someone's attention in the gathering heat. And they will surely come looking, because he is an airman and too important to be forgotten.

The only thing is to roll him into the water. That way when they find him there's a chance people will believe he has drowned accidentally – perhaps fell backwards and hit his head on the bridge. I doubt it, but it is the best I can think of. He is too heavy for me to move any distance by myself, else I'd dig a grave in among the trees. William would be a help, but I should not involve him further; he didn't realise what he was doing, it's no one's fault but mine. Besides, David's body would not stay buried long before the police came with their dogs to pick through the woods. Mrs Heckleton or some other interferer in the village is bound to have seen us walking together and will have tipped them off. And if they were to find him in the ground they'd know for certain it was not an innocent mistake. And I'd have to confess everything.

I don't care about the rest of them, they can think what they like. I don't even mind admitting to Kate, though I no longer need her to know the pointlessness of betrayal. No, when they uncover what we were doing together and everyone thinks me dirt, I'm strong enough to ignore their outrage; I can put up with all of it. Everything except Tom finding out. I couldn't bear him to get me wrong and think I did it to spite him, when I only did it because of the unknowing.

All these thoughts are crazing me too much so I drop to my knees and try to hitch up his trousers to cover his bareness. It is a struggle to get them buttoned, but somehow I succeed; his shirt is too much though – hopefully people will think he took it off to swim or get some sun.

I start David's body towards the slow-moving current. Leaves stick like leeches to his pinkness, and his sprawling arms catch and slow his progress as I roll his dead weight down the slope. At last, he lies at the edge of the bank. One final effort sends him over the two-foot drop in a shower of spray.

May the water wash away my sin.

WILLIAM

Greyness slips across the window's gouged-out slit of sky as the gloom grows ever blacker. The Air Man was an idiot and my sister a fool for doing it with him. But I am even more stupid for clouting him because the police man who came after Laura died will detect my guilt from a mile off. I will be taken away to Norwich Prison and fed nothing but bread and water while they decide what to do. If only Rachel can keep quiet and help me hide his body a chance remains no one will ever find out, because I do not think they will uncover him if we put him in the part of the wood where me and him caught the cock pheasant – where the little babes were murdered – that spot is too dark to search for long and the shadows lie too thick.

A noise down the stairs: shuffling at the door.

'Is there anybody there?'

Rachel. She has come to turn me in. I knew she would tell no lies for me; now I am finished. I cross my fingers she will not climb the steps because I have to see *him* again. I need him to come back, because he always knows the right thing to do. More shuffling, before her plunging footfalls brush away along the path.

She has gone; I will wait.

I wedge myself small into the corner of the room, so he will not be surprised when he returns. If this is a second chance for the two of us to be together I promise not to forget even one word he says, and never once to fail him again.

No watch in my pocket, no time. How many endless, empty minutes? Suddenly a cream-brown shadow and white-wafting wings; his squared-off body stretching itself out on the rafter.

'Are you you?' I ask, and he stares at me from deep within those bottomless hollows, words on the tip of his pointed tongue.

'The Reverend said you would be changed, but he usually is a liar. I got it wrong.'

He stays silent but I can tell he is taking in everything.

'I looked after them, like you said. Only I hit the Air Man with a branch and killed him.'

On his beam against the deadening sky, he perches magnificent and sleek, his transformation final.

'What should I do?'

Beak held wide he coughs his face towards the floor, then jerks it back up to the ceiling like he is trying to shake out words. I do not move one inch, never more ready to listen.

His throat croaks and hisses, edging out a hard lump beyond his hooked tip, which falls onto the floor below. I scramble to my feet, towards where it drops – too quick again – his head spins round and he is gone through the space to the sky.

'Stay! Please!' I shout after him, but too late. On my hands and knees I pick up the pellet that he spat, hoping for a message inside; I break open its oily skin of fur.

Nothing but gristle and bone.

All lies, I think: there is no glorious transformation. Because as his only son he loved me like the world, and if the Reverend's words were true he would have told me what to do. Would have given me a sign of some sort, even if he could not speak.

The owl is just an owl.

He is still buried beneath the churchyard's black loam, churning dust all that remains of him now.

Dazed, I rise. Pausing at the foot of the stairs, fat tears scorch my cheeks and sobs hiccup from my throat. The beam spanning the space above, solid but dotted with beetle holes, remains unchanged since that day. Next door, the wooden chair still mocks me. I kick it over and stamp down hard, splitting the seat before smashing the rest against the wall. I no longer mind it was once his, because if it had not been here none of this would have happened.

And if I had done things different that day, I could have stopped it all.

Firstly, I should not have been at church, but he said it was good for me to go, to keep Mother happy. And when Mrs Heckleton kept me talking afterwards I should not have stayed but ran back quicker. Then I would have met him and we would have gone wandering – nothing bad would have happened and the whole idea would have been forgotten.

But when I get home he has already left, so I change out of my church clothes and head off on my own. I potter round the meadow, stopping to chase butterflies that skitter above the tall grass. I do not plan to enter his house because I hate to go there ever since the lady's voice. For once, though, I stop nearby to listen to a willow warbler. Although I cannot spy its yellow-green body among the pale spring shoots, from beyond the source of its down-slurring song comes a sound from that place. At first I am startled – it might be them again – before I recognise his coughing and grin at myself for being such a coward.

I sneak towards the building's square shadow and, from the undergrowth, watch him inside the doorway. He is standing on top of a chair and his arms are fiddling with something above his head; I cannot see what he is up to because the ivy obscures his face. I suppose he must be fixing the frame so it is less likely to fall down – this is the house where he was born, so I know it is dear to him. Usually when he works at home in the shed – if he is carving an animal out of a piece of wood, or mending something for Mother – he whistles a tune. Now though he must really be concentrating because, apart from the occasional cough, he remains silent. He steps down and emerges, whole, in the doorway, his black hair shining as he moves between the mottled shadows. I am sure he has spotted me, but he turns and vanishes into the room at the side.

I use the opportunity to come closer. After a minute or two his feet appear and climb onto the chair again, toes pointing out towards me. I wonder whether he has nearly finished, or if I should offer to help, but I do not because I gave him my word that I would not come back to this place. From where I am hiding, I can see he has knotted a rope around the beam. And now he is looping the end over his head.

This is not right, I realise, rushing forwards as he bounces on his tiptoes, his feet knocking aside the chair and kicking into the empty space before him. Shouting, I grab his legs and push upwards; my noise subsides, though still he struggles.

'What you doing?' His voice croaks.

'Saving you.'

'Let go now.'

I do not answer because it is difficult to keep his weight off the rope with the way he flaps and beats his arms.

'William, I'm ordering you. Off!'

'Take out your knife. Cut the rope,' I urge him.

He kicks again and I almost lose him until I steady my hold; only my arms are starting to tire because he is so big.

'Promise me,' he whispers, his black eyes peering into my strained face. 'You're the head of the family now. Look after your mother and your sisters.'

And when I say the two words he lifts his hands and grabs the beam, taking the pressure off my burning shoulders.

'I promise.'

He has changed his mind, I think, and relax for a second, trying to hook the fallen-over chair towards me with my leg. 'Hang on,' I say, but already I am too late: he snaps himself earthward again, jerking and twitching so hard I cannot get a hold. His eyes are away somewhere else as I manage to stand the chair upright, stepping up on it and fumbling the bone-handled knife from inside his jacket pocket, then sawing the blade through the rope so he crashes into the empty entrance space, his head snapping back hard against the stairs, so that blood starts to seep.

I think his sprawled body must be gone and touch his bleached cheek. One scared eye flickers as he whispers.

'She can't... Can't be with him.'

'Who?' A ray of sunlight illuminates his face as his chest rises and falls in exaggerated rasps. 'Who do you mean?'

But he does not reply and now I can tell it is too late because he appears different: a sucked-out version of himself. I paw at his face, but his body has gone still. The knot is firm and my tear-wet fingers do not work right as I try to unloop the rope. At last I get it and prop his back against the stairs, buttoning up the collar of his shirt to hide the broken red line around his neck. Then I close his eyelids so he can have some peace. I stand on the chair, stretching up to cut away the other twisted length of rope wrapped around the beam, shoving both pieces up inside the chimney next door before placing the chair neatly alongside the fire.

Silence swells the room as I gulp the stillness. When I have calmed a little I know what I must do and step around his feet to plant a kiss, like Judas in the Bible, on his forehead.

I SHOULD HAVE BEEN BIGGER, I SHOULD HAVE BEEN.

155

I cry out, before climbing beyond where he is slumped, stamping my foot into the stairs so that the floorboards give way and fall back into the cavity below.

Branches snap against my face as I run blindly through the trees. I ignore Mother in the garden and head straight for the farm. A voice inside my chest starts up as I bang on the door.

'He has had an accident! Please!'

And I hurry Mr Marsham and Big Jack to where I left him propped, telling them how he was showing me where he was born when he tripped on a broken step and plummeted. Doctor Howell arrives an hour later and gives me a funny look as he and Big Jack struggle to carry him back to our front room where Mrs Marsham is crying and trying to comfort Mother and my sisters, who sit in terrible silence. Later, the Doctor takes me walking and starts asking about the mark on his neck. My eyes start to fill and I start to cry and shout until he tells me that I should not worry because I have done a good thing for my mother so she will not have to be so sad, and that he will tell no one and make sure that everything is all right, as long as I can stick to my guns and clam up if anyone asks me how it happened. I just have to do one little private thing for him that will stay our secret.

It is a TRAGEDY and everyone in the village nods respectfully at me for the next few days, old ladies offering me sweets, and the men from the farm ruffling my hair – even though I squirm away – and calling me a brave lad. And I almost do manage to forget what has really taken place, until I hear the Reverend's words and watch them lowering the ropes.

Tick-tick. Tick-tap.

I jerk at the sound: not the beat of my heart, but all about me in the rafters, surrounding me, so I can sense their beetle heads watching. This must be the noise he heard; the deathwatches are telling me to join him. Because what is the point of anything if he is not around no more to show me?

A tangle of binding twine is buried in my pocket. If I double up and loop it into a knot it will serve nearly as good as the rope he used. Only, unlike then, there is no one else here to make me stop. I run down the stairs, but at the bottom realise I cannot stand on the chair because I stamped and smashed it. It will not matter – if I climb onto the beam and lie across I can still tie the twine tight.

I mount the first four steps and jump, grabbing the pock-marked timber and raising myself so my elbows hook over the front, my legs dangling. I start to make a loop, only my fingers are trembling so much I cannot tie a proper knot and the twine twists to the floor. As I retrieve it, I cannot stop crying like a baby. If I join with him, no one will be left behind to be the man and look out for my mother and my sisters. And though I will be close to him again, will I even know anything about it, lying lifeless down there in the dirt? Perhaps I should not listen to them, because they are just insects.

Only, he did. So I should follow.

I jump across and cling to the beam once more and, this time, manage to coil the twine. One, two, three loops around till it feels good and strong. I make a circle with the piece that hangs down, just wide enough to fit over my head. My fingers no longer shaking, I tie a slip-knot, pulling it tight against the flesh of my neck. This is the moment. I am ready.

Tap-tick, tick-tock.

And I drop.

THE AIR MAN

A blurring. Everything jerky, like the action in the silent pictures we used to watch at The Globe. Orange and black all around and a flickering below. I'm wedged tight, my eyes half-shut, watching the curtains slowly part until the smell staggers me upright and I look across at Sarge lying on the floor.

It dawns on me: flames are peeling back the fabric covering the fuselage.

Sarge is bloodied and dead, I realise, as I struggle over his body to the cockpit – inside, Skipper and Walter are goners too and Jack's gurgling blood from the corner of his mouth, holding his hands in front of his face like he's trying to figure out what has happened to all the skin that's hanging from his fingers like bright-pink bunting. The Wellington's arc steepens as she ditches towards the shimmering black-red below; my parachute's back in my turret – too late anyhow, I'm anchored here. Not enough time.

Never enough time.

I sit beside Jack, whose eyes have now closed. 'Hang in there, old pal,' I say. 'We ain't ready to go yet.'

But we're falling fast, until we hit the churning surface hard as concrete, shooting below the cold dark drink, which pours in like thunder and sings to us, calling the five of us down, down.

Now the others are swimming about, holding my hand and pulling me beneath the foam while their burnt-out faces beckon me into the blackness.

Everything dizzy and dark and then it is there, sparkling in front of me. Glistening: a golden bracelet at the edge of my reach, floating through the swirling grey. I snatch towards it, but it sinks away and my desperate, empty hands can't find any trace. I try to shout but no sound will come; instead drowning water coughs from my lungs.

I am risen.

She's standing open-mouthed above me, like she's part of the overhanging tree. My head's ropey – I rub it and my fingers come back sticky and dark. I'm not sure what's happening 'cause the branches are swaying and I'm unsteady on my feet;

only, this doesn't seem like how buying it ought to feel. I pull myself up the bank, dirt clumped to my legs, my brain throbbing like a clapped-out diesel. She don't say anything, and I can't as my teeth are chattering so much. So bloody cold.

I struggle with my shirt, but my arms won't go through the holes. I just want to lay up and get some kip. Sleep and forget. Forget all of it – especially her.

She comes across, reaching out towards my flinching, throbbing head. I stumble back, clumsy as a toddler.

'You're not...' she says, flatly.

My fingers are finally through the sleeves and now I can concentrate on the blurred buttons, but her voice jars me to look at her again, my sight no longer so fogged.

'Fuck this for a game of soldiers,' I say, heading off quick as my wavering legs will carry me, the pulsing in my head growing louder and louder.

These Abreharts are welcome to each other.

WILLIAM

Tightness chokes me so I cannot breathe, then a splintering pain in my elbow and I am among the dirt on the floor. Beside me lies the unravelled knot, which gave way when I plunged. The place is silent except for my crying-turned-laughter. Not now, the house and the deathwatches and the owl are telling me. Not now.

I will carry on being the man, as I promised. Because if I were to follow him into the ground, who else would remember everything we did?

Like the nightingale and the pheasants and the fishing and the woods. And Grandfather and all them others I never even saw but he talked about and, sometimes, I feel I can touch. Or Laura and my mother and my sisters.

Instead, I must punish the Reverend for giving me the stupid inkling with his lies. He should be stopped from handing out falseness when the only thing is what is here and now – all those beloved people waiting under the ground can never change into something glorious. I will show everyone what a bloody liar he is, even if it is my last act before they take me away for what I have done to the Air Man.

Dusk's descent is complete and everywhere is changed: the gravestones indistinct, their words unreadable. A bat skitters on angled wings against the blue-black. Sometimes it comes lower, right in front of my face, its mouth snapping shut around flying things that are invisible to my straining eyes – the only sound other than the breeze which stirs the long grass at my feet and the boughs of the elms that overhang the path. Now a distant rumble: another bomber passing somewhere above the round tower, but this time I know the Air Man is not crouching stupidly aboard.

A field of lies surrounds me. Inscriptions offering broken promises of eternity or sleep, when so much less is really given – no other-place reconciliations, no sweet hereafter, no glorious transformations still to come. Not for people like us.

The ancient headstone closest to me leans like a cripple, the shrinking peat below sending it halfway horizontal. I kick my boot against it to help it on its way. Nothing gives, so I stamp again and again, until it wobbles over with a soft thud. Nearby stands the headless angel. I take a loose lump of flint from the floor and use it to knap at its wing, shearing off the tip before smashing away the rest, till just the useless torso remains. Another memorial falls under my force and I toss the flint high through one of the darkened windows, piercing the glass with a sharp crack – not the explosion of shards I am hoping for to wake the Reverend from his house across the way.

I stand over his sticks and fall to the ground, clutching at their spindly insignificance as I bury my nostrils in the grass, its dampness masking my tears. My fingernails split as I claw at the soil, bringing up handfuls of musty earth: still not close enough to catch his smell. I dig down deeper, wanting more than anything to see and touch what remains of him, but my hands struggle with the ground's hardness and I collapse, spent, way above where he lies in his box.

A roar in my throat comes bubbling up again and this time it will not stop. It rumbles deep into the earth before I lift my head and it obscures all other sound in the world.

It is everywhere.

Weaving through the rugged elms.

Up in the tower among the smoothed-over devil faces that goad me with their soundless shrieks.

Even filling the sky itself.

'COME BACK. PLEASE. COME BACK. YOU HAVE TO.'

An uncountable spell, then I hear what sounds like a fox snuffling, so rise and follow the noise around to the rear of the churchyard. A figure in black – a lady, I think – stands in the open space at the far corner, her back towards me. She could have been here the whole time and I would not have realised because, apart from the snuffling – which now I realise must be her softly sobbing – she makes little sound. I move closer and she turns.

'William?'

It is Mother. She holds out a hand and I grab it. She is different out here, her face seems softer in the starlight than it does around the house. Now I realise why she sits and stares so much: she must miss him like I do. I know because her face is red-raw:

161

she has been crying like anything. In her other hand she carries a bunch of tulips.

'Why you here?' I ask. 'His is round the other side.' I expect her to be surprised by the sound of my voice, but she does not seem to notice.

'Not him. I'm here for someone else. You'd a sister called Hope. Only, when she was born, she was too little.'

'Hope,' I repeat, the word hanging unsteady in the air because I am still not used to speaking. 'Like Laura.'

'Two years older than Rachel she'd be. I never said as you were too small and your father didn't want talk of her. Here, help me.' We take the flowers together and place them against the wall, where their purple petals will catch the light of the mid-morning sun.

'It's fine to miss him, William. But you shouldn't make him into something he wasn't. He was no saint – he was hollow.'

If anyone else said this I would be angry and storm off, but I have used it all up tonight and just feel cold and shivery. Perhaps that is what she means. Perhaps, all of us Abreharts are hollowed-out and wrong inside.

She stumbles suddenly, her left arm stiffening as she grimaces at the sky. I help her down to the damp grass, resting her other hand on my shoulder. Her face looks pale, even in this nothing-light.

'What's wrong?'

'I'll be alright. Give me a minute.'

She hoists herself to her feet, using me as a leaning post. Once up, her arm relaxes a little and she tries to smile.

'Someone's walked over my grave, that's all. I'll head home.'

But she does not move anywhere for a minute or two, her fingers squeezing my arm, her mouth sucking in gutfuls of grass-washed air. Now the queerness has passed and she seems a little better.

'You follow when you're ready, William. Don't worry about me.'

As she turns I tug on her sleeve.

'Why do bad things always happen to us?'

She looks like she is going to answer, but does not.

Part of my head wants to share the secret, so I am no longer the only one who knows that what happened by the stairs was no accident. Doctor Howell does not count, because he said if I did the thing he would never say to anyone else. But, as I think about telling her, I picture the funeral-look on his face as he slumped there; the Air Man's limp body joins him in my head, grinning at me with a skeleton's sneer so that I am certain that no one else should find out.

'Mother, I done something wrong.'

'It's alright, William.'

'Kate's Air Man. I killed him.'

'Shush. It's late. Things will seem different in daylight.'

She kisses me on the forehead and begins tottering unsteadily up the path, disappearing then reappearing as she moves beneath the deep shadow-pools cast by the trees. A perfect silence surrounds me now, a silence not even disturbed by the subtle snapping of the bat overhead, and I picture the little girl I never knew about: another one like Laura, only Hope *was* my sister and not my niece. It is empty: all these people under the grass, with so few of us left knowing that once they were real walking men and women, or even tiny babies crawling in the sunlit world. One day soon – when the police men come and take me away – I will be in darkness too. Who or what will remember anything about me?

Nothing but the birds and the trees.

I go back around to the front of the church, ashamed now by the flatness of the gravestones I kicked over. As I try to stand them upright, he flickers into my mind – like the way pictures fill the space behind your eyes when you are reading a book and each new page is turned:

Silhouetted on the crest of a field, the wind blowing steady at his back. He holds his hands aloft and the kite soars way off in the cornflower sky as I run below in circles, retrieving its delicate frame when it crashes to earth, then flinging it in front of me for him to drag skywards, diving and swooping like a giant bird only he can control.

His covered-over anger erupting when Rachel tells him she is expecting, firing out so hard that I wonder: can this be the same man that takes me walking in the woods and fields?

In his best clothes dancing after Alfred Tucker's wedding, spinning first Mrs Morley, then Mrs Marsham round the room, their faces pulled taut into smiles as the crowd whistles and stomps, but me clapping the loudest.

163

Or the dead-look in his eyes as he swings to and fro, to and fro. Before twisting and coming up two years prior with the ten-pound pike he has pulled from the Devil's Pit, which we fry for tea in big buttery chunks that same evening.

All these thoughts and more keep coming at me and I wonder if they will ever stop, or just yellow and vanish like time-faded photographs.

I stumble through the murk. As I approach the bottom of the drove a shape lurches from the verge. Startled I freeze – the thing has the appearance of the Air Man, only it cannot be because I have killed him. It must be his ghost come for revenge – somehow he knows that I was the one that hit him.

'What you looking at, you little shit? Heh?'

And he staggers away, clutching his head and laughing like a lunatic, his hair silver in the moonlight. I watch him disappear into the dark, until I am sure he is not coming back. I did not murder him after all, I realise, just knocked him out flat. Relief flows through me – this proves I was not ready to be strung up for everyone to gawp at, because it is an awful thing and I did not want people to watch me swinging and kicking.

Nobody should have to see that.

I unfasten the front door and prise off my boots. Inside it is blacker still, but my sight is accustomed. Mother is at the table; she gives me a scare because she sits so quiet.

'Night-night,' I say, but she does not reply and I think at first she must have dozed off, only her eyes are wide. Her mouth opens, finally, in a whisper.

'Fetch your sisters, William.'

In the room's monotonous tint there is something wrong about her face – even more so than in the churchyard. I run upstairs and shove open the door to their room. Kate's bed is empty; Rachel is emerging from hers, sleep-starved and scowling.

'Mother says to come.'

She must still be mad with me from before and the Air Man – perhaps she does not yet realise he is alive again – but she does not speak as she follows me down the stairs, only lets out a little gasp when she sees her, the sound stirring Mother to look up.

'William,' Mother whispers, so quiet I can hardly hear. I lean in closer. 'Cling to the good, forget the bad.'

Her face blanches as she speaks. I nod, but do not understand even half of what has happened tonight. And I am no wiser as to why he did that thing he did, because I always tried my best to be how he would have wanted – like I am doing now – so he could not have been disappointed with me, could he? Only I will never find out, I realise: he cannot explain now and neither can Mother. Because even if I told her the truth about him not falling down the stairs and she knew the reason, her eyes are already closing and her chest is moving too slowly.

Just like his did.

I think my breathing will do the opposite and go all quick and panicky again, like when he was slumped beside me, but Rachel is here and this time I stay calm, because the lady before us looks as peaceful as I ever can remember.

'Should we go for the Doctor?' I ask.

'Let's just be quiet for a while.'

And we sit alongside her, Rachel stroking stray hairs from her face, as I grip my hand around my mother's bone-like fingers.

MOTHER

This is a difference I have not felt before; back in myself the world seems my own. I see things stacked up behind me, not like all those jarring moments I could never control. Now I see it all coming up, and everything that has gone before. Not-Louise is me and I am Not-Louise. It should be liberating, though there is something in the difference – a sourness – which lingers in the air like the smell of rotting leaves: I sensed it visiting Hope earlier, when the pain first gripped my chest.

I think my heart is giving up the ghost. Like poor Nan's did, as she dozed in the sickly sunlight, her head slumped against her shoulder when I came to call her inside.

Rachel and William are with me, though Kate is not – a shame, for I should like to see that big smile of hers again. William's eyes, intent as ever, peer into mine searching for answers.

'Cling to the good, forget the bad,' I tell him, because he still has a chance. And, really, that is all we can do.

I search for words for Rachel too, words to give meaning to the passing of her little girl. But nothing I can think of will suffice, even though losing Hope should have gifted me an insight; I have become like John: he, too, knew there were no words.

Knew it all along.

Louise wanders the woods looking for primroses to pick. Rachel and Kate are back at the cottage playing with their grandfather – William yet to come – as she brushes past the saplings of ash which guard the ruined house: the place she entered with John soon after they met, when everything was awash with promise.

She plucks the soft yellow flowers from where they emerge like fragments of sunshine through the thin litter of leaves. A sound within the walls startles her and she approaches a window: inside the space is barren, just a single wooden chair. She creeps beneath the ivy-clad doorway – a repeat of the first time they kissed – and stands at the bottom of the stairs. Listening.

Nothing to begin with, only the trees and the breeze. Now noises upstairs. Breathing becoming groaning, becoming shouting. Carefully she ascends to the hallway above, pausing beyond the half-open door. Inside, John's bare back rises and falls. *Transfixed, she stands watching. No anger, just surprise at finding him like this. From the doorway she cannot see the face of the woman underneath him, but does not want to move closer in case they notice her. Besides, part of her has no desire to know, no desire to be party to any of this. She slinks away, half-tripping as she descends the narrow stairway, but they do not hear her over John's animal grunting and the woman's shouts.*

During the following months she sometimes feels a compulsion to return, concealing herself further back, among the ferns, because she does not need to bear witness again. Listening is sufficient.

I have never been enough, she thinks, one evening as she lies beneath him, staring at the moonbeams that have pooled in the corner of their bedroom.

'Hollow,' she says, the word bringing a stop to his pinning thrusts.

'What?'

'I'm broken aren't I?'

'You say some things, Louise.'

'I've heard you in that place. I know.'

'Which place?'

'The house in the trees.'

'What you going on about?' He pulls away and sits on the edge of the bed, a hint of guilt, she thinks, in the way his eyes avoid meeting hers directly.

'It doesn't matter,' she continues, 'I know I'm not enough. I'm hollow – like you.'

'Why are you doing this?'

'Hope,' she replies.

But even as she says it, he is pulling on his trousers and stamping down the stairs. She watches him cross the grass and fuse with the night, her head bustling with an explosion of colours as she tries to anchor herself down.

And the same colours move before me now, twisting like the shapes in a child's kaleidoscope:

Kate's primrose-yellow curls.

The black of William and Rachel's eyes, full of flickering shadows and the green-dark woods.

Streaks of purple sweet peas, white carnations and orange marigolds burst at the edge of my senses, gradually washed over with a deep, deep blue, which spreads before me, serene and infinite. Hope is whispering from the blood-red, as John's hollow heart beats closer, ever closer. This is the time, at last. Familiar as rain. The ill luck has run its course.

I will go now, and be gone.

WILLIAM

No dreams came to me in the early hours, even though my fractured sleep was barely real. Once when my eyes eased open in the still-dark, I peered across and hoped she might be up and about in the garden, doing what she loved best, but she was still just sitting there, all rigid. She is in the same place when I awaken, though how could she be anywhere else?

Peaceful. Not like him. As if what has happened was meant to be.

Silence soaks the morning. Kate is sombre as she toasts bread on the fire. Rachel is brewing the tea and my mouth trembles as I realise one less cup will need pouring from here on in. Now Kate notices I am awake and her eyes meet mine.

'Here, get some of this in you.'

She came in as I held Mother's hand in the darkness, screaming blue murder at Rachel.

'What was David doing here?' she shouted. 'I met him up the drove. He was acting all queer, saying it was over between us. You've gone and done something to spoil it, haven't you!'

Then she saw Mother and her voice petered away; I could hear my sisters whispering to each other as I sank towards sleep. I hope the Air Man does not ever come back: if he must I will leave them be, whichever one he ends up with – I tried my best to be the head of the family but it went wrong.

I crunch down my toast at the window because I do not want to eat in sight of Mother's blue-tinged face. Her skin shines like porcelain and, even though Rachel drew her eyelids closed with her thumb – like I did his – it still feels as if she is watching.

'Someone should fetch help,' Rachel says.

I say nothing, but do not really want to see Doctor Howell again after what happened before. Rachel and Kate look like lost souls, though, as they wander about the room, and I promised him I would be the man, which my sisters need now more than ever. Besides, I am bigger and will not do that thing again if the Doctor should ask.

'I will,' I say, half-coughing to clear my throat because it still seems strange when a sound emerges.

'Alright,' says Kate. 'We'll stay with her. Make her look nice.'

169

Into the day and already swifts are shrieking through the white sky-space, a scramble of silhouettes as they squeeze beneath the roof. They seem so excited to be back for their brief summer. What has become of Mother means nothing to them; they lead their own separate lives up there, only touching down for fleeting seconds before they are up again among the clouds.

He was no saint, she said, and she did not mean he was not a religious man like Saint Peter or Saint Paul – more that he had his faults. And I know her words are true, because I remember how he was the evening Rachel announced she was expecting, and the day he gave me a right good hiding when he caught me and Joe pelting conkers into the Marshams' garden – though perhaps I did deserve to cop it, even if I did not chuck many. But all the rest of the time there was nothing bad – he was the strongest man in the village and everybody admired him – you could see it when they lowered the ropes, because the church was packed like I have never seen. Not even at Christmas.

He was kind and brave and strong and fun. And loving too – after Laura died I watched him in secret each afternoon before he returned home from the farm, hunched above her grave, whispering and talking to her. So, even though it is only worms and centipedes down there, at least he is close to his granddaughter now. She must be the reason he did it, because he loved her too much and could not bear that she had gone so small, especially as he was meant to have another little girl – my secret sister – who I know now was taken before time too.

Hope.

I am glad I made it like an accident on the stairs. Else people who were ignorant of the whole would think him a coward, and he WAS NOT. But they would still have lowered him in the churchyard because those other times are long gone. He told me about it when we were walking by the crossroads.

'They used to drive a stake through the bodies of suicides in the old days and bury them here. At midnight.' He puts on a scary expression and wiggles his hands in the air, which makes me laugh because the day is bright and not even a little bit frightening. Besides, it looks like any other crossroads with high hedges and a white signpost.

'What's a suicide?'

170

'Someone who's taken their own life. Killed themself.'

'Why would they?'

'Because they're unhappy about the way things have turned out, I suppose. Or they've done something they want to forget. Though who knows why anyone does anything?'

I nod and he carries on.

'They used to put them where the roads meet so their souls would be confused and unable to find their way back to any people who'd wronged them.'

'That's stupid,' I reply, 'because they'd realise exactly where they were standing if they came from round nearby.'

'Well, people can't have thought of that!' And he laughs.

'You ever know anyone who done it?'

His laughing stops abruptly and he does not answer. We carry on in silence to Summer End, where he is to do some jobs for Mrs Hobbs – another widowed lady he helps out, like Mrs Morley. I am sent packing with her son Peter, who is noisy and scares all the birds, always moaning about it being time to head back, even though we are supposed to stay out for a good long while.

The pair of us come to one of the pits round the back of Summer End Church where I know there is a waterhen's nest, its brown mess of sticks puncturing the film of dead leaves that litter the oily surface. The eggs are out of reach but I still think I can grab one if I lean far enough, though Peter is dead against it. Stretching forward I slip into the cold-black: my feet kicking against the rotted vegetation, my mouth choked full of gulping filth. I somehow haul myself out – Peter no help at all, just repeating to himself this was a bad idea as I scramble up the bank. I leave him there and shiver home, frightening Mother half to death when she sees me. After she recovers from the shock she is livid, which is not like her, her voice almost turning into a shout as she goes on about the idiocy of playing near water. But when he gets back, he thinks it funny that I appear so black and bedraggled. 'Here's a drowned otter,' he says, which has me in fits until Mother makes me fetch the bath out in front of the fire, scrubbing so hard I think the skin behind my ears will peel away down my neck, leaving only raw flesh beneath.

Now I am before the Marshams' door, the third time I have come to telephone for Doctor Howell: first Laura, then him, now Mother. I rap the lion head and wait. Nothing happens for a minute and I think about banging again when there is movement inside.

Ruth Marsham answers, which I do not expect. She is not quite a year younger than me and goes to a different school – near London someplace – where she even has to stay and sleep.

'Hello,' she says. She is dark-haired and tall for a girl; almost, but not quite, as high as me.

'Could you ring for Doctor Howell please?'

She turns and shouts up the stairs. 'Mother! William Abrehart's here to use the telephone.'

I gaze down at all the tiny tiles fitted together on the floor in a pattern like the Romans used to make, because I am embarrassed to look Ruth full in the face, wearing my scruffy clothes. Now Mrs Marsham emerges in a silky white dressing gown and slippers, even though it must be already past eight o'clock.

'What's the matter, William? Come inside. Ruth, fetch William some milk.'

'We need the Doctor. Mother's gone.'

'Gone?' She frowns, and when what I mean dawns on her a noise comes out of her mouth, her hand lifting too late to trap it within.

'Oh! I see,' she says, stumbling towards where the telephone rests on a little table, sitting me down on the chair beside before opening the drawer and getting out a book. She dials the number with a shaky finger.

'Doctor Howell? Hello, it's Rosamond Marsham... Hello. Would it be possible for you to come over? It's rather urgent I'm afraid. William Abrehart has just turned up... Yes, their mother... I'm not sure exactly... Would you like a word with him?'

She hands me the bit you talk into and listen at, and whispers that I should explain what has happened. I do not much want to talk to him but realise I must. As I speak I am aware of her – and Ruth – staring at me, which makes my cheeks go hot. The Doctor talks very slow and clear at the other end of the telephone: he will be over presently. I pass it back to Mrs Marsham. She says some more into it then places it down.

'William, I'm so sorry.'

172

I do not know what to do next, so just stand there.

'I'll come as soon as I'm dressed. Would you like Ruth to walk back with you?'

I nod and the pair of us go outside, turning right onto the lane, past the dark clump of ivy that has claimed their wall for itself. Not even a single sparrow is chittering in the hedge, though after a while she fills the still air with her posh-sounding voice.

'What does she look like? Aren't you scared?'

'As if she is sleeping.' And we go on in silence. When we reach the edge of our garden she starts to turns back.

'I hope everything gets sorted out,' she says, touching me lightly on the hand.

'Thank you,' I say.

Not much has changed inside, except now Kate is putting pinkness onto Mother's mouth and has painted her cheeks to make them more coloured. If anything, though, she seems less alive: something is wrong about it all because I hardly remember her wearing that stuff, apart from the odd special service in church.

We do not have to wait long until the door is rattling. It is too soon for Doctor Howell so I presume it will be Mrs Marsham. Rachel opens it and straightaway I hear his voice: the Reverend, all hot air and wringing hands as he comes through to the kitchen. Mrs Marsham must have told him.

'So sorry for your loss,' he says sombrely, nod-bowing to each of us in turn.

'Reverend,' Rachel replies. I stare into his little beady eyes.

'Was it peaceful?' he says, as he studies Mother where she sits.

'Yes.'

'Good, good. That is a blessing.'

I cannot help myself, anger spewing out of my mouth. 'It is not. SHE IS GONE!'

He seems surprised for a moment, not by my actual words so much, but more because I am talking – SHOUTING – again. I think he is actually quite pleased, probably believing that now he will be able to chat with me about miracles and glories, and all the rest of it.

'You're right, William. Though I didn't mean in that sense – more that, perhaps, we can be thankful your mother will now find the peace absent within her for so long.'

I do not respond, my head boiling away, staring out the window at a wood pigeon that flaps in an upward arc above the trees.

'Your mother can now receive His Mercy.'

'No! Dead is all.' My cheeks are damp as I turn on him and I can tell Kate and Rachel hardly dare look at me.

'You do not hardly know anything about her so you should not say what she might want. YOU STUPID BLOODY LIAR!'

His bottom lip vibrates a little, like a quivering bluebottle chafing its wings before flight, and I storm outside, passing Mrs Marsham on the grass before going along the path between the trees, where I start to run and do not stop. I carry straight on past his house, across the meadow, because I am not ready to go there again yet.

In any case, I should leave the owl to his day-sleep.

Instead, I hurry to the lush grass by the watercress and rest down my head, feeling more tired than I ever can remember.

Beside me, my mother kneels in a glade surrounded by flowers; not all sad like at a funeral, but blinding and beautiful. She is laughing in the way she used to when I was small – the way that would make cackling magpies out of me, Rachel and Kate: a sound I must always try to recall.

Looking beyond, through the trees, I notice a figure half-hidden among the ferns and nettles, beckoning me to follow.

Him.

I turn to ask Mother, but she has gone so I sneak from the clearing. The two of us walk in silence for hours – cool below the wood's cavernous shelter – like none of the bad things have happened. But as I stare into his owlish eyes, I already sense his face growing fuzzier under the emerald shade, and I realise: each day will add to his obscurity, until all that persists is a stubborn shadow that stalks the deepest hollows of my imagination.

I awake with a start; the wind has taken on a bitter edge and the meadow stretches away, colourless beneath the desolate sky.

May 5th 1945

MRS HECKLETON

Besides the familiarity of the usual faces it's an odd spectacle in here, carnival-like with all of them in the far aisle, spruced up so smart in their uniforms. The noise they make with their chattering and larking about, I can't follow what they're going on about half the time! Such lovely young men, and polite too, always calling out in those funny voices whenever they pass me in the village. I'll be sorry to see them go, but will forever be grateful for the way they've put their lives on the line for our freedom, bringing the fighting's end so very close. Because any day soon it will surely be over, now Hitler has got what was coming to him. The times these past few years I've had to traipse here to listen to the Reverend deliver one painful eulogy after another, while those poor mothers and wives sat wailing up front. Today's different, thank heavens: the groom alongside one of his pals, glancing about with the widest of grins.

The main door swings open and they approach the altar. William's at her side, tall as his father and nearly as broad-shouldered: the double of him in that jacket. She's dressed white as the walls, a veil hanging down so I can't see her face. Must be over the moon to have snagged such a handsome one; you'd never credit it with everything life's thrown at them, but that family's nothing if not resilient. Was a surprise to find the wedding happening here – I quite expected it to be a shotgun affair. Where she managed to get such a dress from I'll never know, but I suppose the Yanks have the ways and means to get round the coupons.

The organ gets going and the pair start up the aisle. I'm happy things have come good for her, I really am. She's proved people wrong with how she's knuckled down.

Her sister looks better than of late too, sitting up front on her own. Now the Hall's a hospital it's a real service she's doing to nurse those unfortunates who didn't make it home in one piece. I'm sure it's kept her mind off everything these last years – must be lonely in that house without her mother, even if poor Louise hadn't been exactly all there for longer than I can remember. How she'll cope with only William for company when the new bride goes to America, only time will tell. But I suppose she must be getting used to it by now, what with her sister away with the WAAF and hardly ever home. Still, she's got an old head on young shoulders; I dare say she'll get by, though it's bound to be a body blow.

At least her brother has grown up better than anyone could have hoped. The way he would lurk so sullen and silent always put the wind up me; then the incident in the graveyard with the headstones and smashed windows. The Reverend suspected him, but was too Christian to make a fuss after what had happened that same night to Louise. Not that the lad isn't still a strange one, wandering the woods every spare minute of the day, but by all accounts he's a good worker at the farm, even if he does keep himself to himself. Looked happy as a cat in a hen coup when I watched him driving his tractor the other day, that mop of black hair flicking in front of his face as he ploughed up and down the field in perfect straight lines.

Here comes the bride! How lovely she looks, almost floating above the aisle in those satiny shoes and long, trailing dress. She'll need to be sure not to get too ahead of herself when she's over there, though, and remember where she's from. If only Louise's heart hadn't given up – she would have loved watching her daughter tying the knot, decked out so prettily.

Rachel seems proud of her sister, but I dare say she's wondering what might have been. I used to think she was a bit of a one – always some drama or other – but there's been nothing untoward since her poor little one. I knew all along it was hers, though it was nice of Louise to pretend, to try and take the shame. I still wouldn't mind betting it was Tom Morley, God rest him, who got her in trouble, before running off to avoid the consequences; poor lad chose the wrong time to join up, though, what with the war only a year-and-a-bit away. Still, far as I can tell Rachel doesn't show much interest in any of that any more. It's a surprise considering the number of admirers she's had, but they all get the same short shrift. Not like Kate – wouldn't have shocked me if she'd got through a whole regiment once she was posted off and surrounded by all those eager suitors – though even she hasn't been without her tribulations. That time she screamed blue murder when they broke the news to her about

the airman she was so keen on at the beginning of the fighting –
the one whose aeroplane went down over the North Sea only a
day or two after their mother passed. She tried to put on a brave
show, but I could tell it hit her hard. Was no bad thing when
they put the call out to women and she went off to be among
new faces – something to keep her mind from dwelling.

No, it's good they're getting a bit of happiness, after all the
funerals and rotten luck. Were I the superstitious sort, I'd have
started to wonder before now that there wasn't some curse
hovering over them, what with all the accidents and tragedies.
But I don't hold with that sort of thing: you create your own
path through life and have to face the consequences of your
actions.

No, Rachel and William are as well off left to their own
devices, getting on quietly with things without any complications
in the way.

Not that I'd ever be one to say anything, of course.

RACHEL

Just because five years have passed does not mean the worst.

Not necessarily.

Although there has been no word, and nobody says it to my face, I can tell they all think that Tom isn't coming back. But they're wrong. With the Germans ready to surrender, things will soon start to clear up; thousands of prisoners must be left adrift over there in the chaos. I'm certain he's waiting, desperate to return to where he belongs. Because if the unspeakable had happened I'd know.

I would have sensed something.

Any day soon, news of his liberation will come, then hardly any time at all before he is home and we can get on with the rest of our life together – the way things were meant to be. Like what Kate will have from now on with her Jimmy.

My ivory sister steps down the aisle, her dress shimmering in the streaming sunlight. She turns to me, her face blurred beneath the veil. I smile, though I can tell this is the last day my eyes will look upon hers, and it is all I can do to stop the trickle of tears from becoming a flood. Once she has left for America it will be for good. One parting will be all; I know she won't ever return. When I lay with David it changed things. And though we remain sisters, it cannot go back between us like it was.

I will miss her too much, but part of me is relieved: she can finally get away from this place. She won't have to be a statue any longer.

No, until Tom comes back it will just be William and me. He's looking all grown-up wearing Father's suit, though I still see a hint of that strange, silent boy in his eyes: they're darting round the congregation as he hands Kate across to her groom. Now he shuffles alongside me, and the Reverend starts his solemnities, welcoming us all into His house.

'We are gathered here...'

His words drone past my head and I am not thinking of this church, or this ceremony, but of Tom and all the things – the wonderful things – we will do when he returns and rescues me from my hiding place.

Wading through the exquisite coldness of the water to that thick palace of overhanging willow, thousands of sounds will envelop us as I cradle Laura in my arms: the three of us hypnotised by the hiss of the wind, the trickle of the stream, and the hum of the world around us.

Everything indivisible, merging into one. The way it was always meant to be.

WILLIAM

Kate is a white swan next to her Yank, who does not seem too much of an idiot. But however beautiful my sister looks, she is not the prettiest girl in the church: I grin down the aisle, past Rachel alone out front, to Ruth Marsham two pews back. She gives me a smirk no one else sees before glancing away; none of them have any idea about us. Her father, to her left, wears his usual bored expression. He keeps taking his watch out of his pocket and checking it – everything always on the clock – though Mrs Marsham seems pleased to be here, smiling and chatting to the people around her. I hope I can meet Ruth later, if she can sneak off from the party and the games without anyone realising; I know a place we can go.

Thurtle tells us to be seated, so I make my way next to Rachel. He goes on in that manner of his which slows time so, giving me a black look every so often. I ignore him, my mind running through the things I will show her, until the sombre words stop and Kate and the Yank are kissing by the altar. Then Rachel and me are in the vestry to bear witness, watching them fill in the book before we print our own names: William Abrehart, May Fifth Nineteen Forty-five.

Outside everyone laughs as rose confetti swirls about us like the hawthorn blossom that will fall in the next few weeks, showering my sister and her new Air Man. I concentrate on one petal that is blowing across the churchyard, swept high on a gust before going gently to ground above his grave.

The marble of his stone is jet black, like the colour of his hair; I saved my wages from the farm and put them together with Rachel's and Kate's until we could afford it. Mother is beside him too, their names inscribed in gold letters:

John Thomas Abrehart and Louise Abrehart
Beloved Father and Mother

'She'd have liked being here today,' Rachel says, appearing at my side.

Her face seems sad in the harsh afternoon light, her skin off-white and strained by all the dragging days nursing at the Hall, and the evenings she stays with her ear pinned to the wireless, waiting for news of Tom.

Always listening.

Fretting for nothing, because he surely died five years ago, though she will not admit it to anyone, least of all herself. Even Mrs Morley seems resigned; sometimes I notice her laying flowers for her lost son beside the church wall. She stands there now, observing events from a distance. Not a witch, I realise, just a lonely woman.

A car coasts up and Kate shouts us across. We follow, everywhere jokes and laughter, Yank accents filling the sky. I pull my face taut too, but feel no elation as my sister climbs in, waving like this is the last goodbye – though I will see her one more time at the party later before she goes away for good. Through the riot of faces Ruth's dark eyes catch mine and she smiles as the car rattles down the lane.

The crowd swirls around the doorway, unsure what to do. I feel hot and head-heavy, a sudden need to be away from all the loudness, to immerse myself in my thoughts. Rachel has wandered towards the back corner of the churchyard; I should not disturb her because, even though her and me share this thing, we are both of us separate, and nothing I say can make any of it better.

But there is something I can do.

I slide away, furtive, so that no one even knows I have left, hurrying across the meadow to his house. The roof and ceiling are closer to nothingness than before, the stones beneath the ivy-clad walls no longer visible. Inside is empty and cool – a cathedral to the sky – offering only scant shelter for the animals and insects that come here. Everywhere whiffs of mushrooms and musty earth, of unstoppable decay.

Warily up the stairs, careful not to let my smart shoes puncture the rotten timber. At the top lies a precarious bridge of floorboards, which bows under my weight like the plank that crosses the watercress beds. I peer through the doorway but cannot see his white outline in its usual place. He still comes here now and then – last year he nested in the broken chimney breast, fledging three click-hissing young – but I have not seen him for more than a month. Perhaps he has grown too old and died, because he must be a right good age for an owl. In any case, even if he is still about he will be all right: there are other places nearby for him to go.

Back downstairs I study the cheerless walls, straining one final time to catch the voices Rachel told me of an age ago.

Silence.

And I realise with an empty certainty that there is nothing but the now-time – nothing but this moment – which I have to make stand for something.

I pick what remains of the chair off the floor and stack the spindles of wood in the centre of the room, before ferreting up around inside the chimney: his rope is still where I left it. I drop it onto the growing pile, adding big handfuls of wind-blown sticks that have hoarded themselves in the room's corners. Pulling out a match from my pocket, I strike it against the hearthstone: an amber flame hisses, sparking when I touch it to the makeshift kindling. We have been waterless this past week so it takes well, and soon a good fire is going; already the rope has fizzled away, the shattered ribs of the chair transforming into bright red embers. I pile on more sticks, scattering them over the floor. In no time they are alight, the flames reaching across the room. Now I remove his jacket and fling it on top. I watch for a moment, but soon the heat becomes too much and I have to step outside. The blaze burns angrily, yet the fever is hemmed into that square space, held back by the greenness of the gathered leaves and branches. It will not take long for the house to be consumed, for the peeled-back wallpaper to ignite and the beetle-wasted boards to blacken; not long for every trace to be gone, all save the stones that, in time, will subside to lie in secret, choked by nettles and briars.

A ghost house of a different kind.

I turn away, only stopping to look back when I reach the meadow's edge; I do not watch for long because the rising sparks remind me of the bonfires him and me used to make together, so gleeful, in the garden.

From the far woods, faint echoes of birdsong float on the breeze. I head towards the direction of their sound, towards the distant trees. I am ready now, ready to whisper my words to them.

Listen. Do you hear?

A NOTE ON BIRD NAMES

One of the main themes of *The Listeners* is loss, and this is reflected by much of the wildlife encountered by William. Many of the birds, as well as some of the trees and other wildlife that are mentioned have, since 1940, become much scarcer in the county – and in the case of the 'butcher-bird', have disappeared entirely (no longer a UK breeding species, the last Norfolk pair nested in the Brecks in 1988).

As well as the actual loss of Norfolk's once-common avifauna, many of the names given to the county's birds have also fell out of usage. I have tried to redress this by using old English and Norfolk dialect bird names throughout the novel where I thought it appropriate, though because William is quite the amateur naturalist he often uses familiar common names, rather than some of the really esoteric local ones I could have given to him! Below is a list of some of the less obvious featured names:

Butcher-bird – Red-backed Shrike
Harnser – Grey Heron
Little black-and-white woodpecker – Lesser Spotted Woodpecker
Peewit – Lapwing
Screech owl, white owl – Barn Owl
Storm-cock – Mistle Thrush
Waterhen – Moorhen
Yaffle – Green Woodpecker

To help research these archaic names and the stories associated with them, I consulted a number of sources, which are an excellent read for anyone interested in the subject:

Cocker, M. and Mabey, R., *Birds Britannica*, London, Chatto & Windus, 2005.
Greenoak, F., *British Birds: their Folklore, Names and Literature*, London, Helm, 1997.
Lockwood, W. B., *The Oxford Dictionary of British Bird Names*, Oxford, Oxford University Press, 1993.

In addition, useful information was gained from asking some older Norfolk residents about their recollections of various local names, and from a paper entitled 'Richard Richardson's List of Norfolk Bird Names' compiled by Richard Fitter and published in the *Norfolk Bird and Mammal Report 2004*.

A number of publications were also very useful to check on the changing distribution of the county's birds including:

Norfolk Bird and Mammal Report, and the earlier *Norfolk Bird Report* and *Wild Bird Protection in Norfolk*. Various, all pub. by Norfolk and Norwich Naturalists' Society.

Holloway, S., *The Historical Atlas of Breeding Birds in Britain and Ireland 1875–1900*. London, T. & A. D. Poyser, 1996.

Taylor, M., Seago M., Allard P., & Dorling, D., *The Birds of Norfolk*. Bexhill on Sea, Pica Press. 1999.

ACKNOWLEDGEMENTS

Many people helped and encouraged me during the writing of *The Listeners*, and I am grateful to all of them. In particular, I'd like to thank my fellow workshop students on the Creative Writing MA at the University of East Anglia, where the novel began way back in September 2006, with special mention to Chris Rose and Dan Timms for reading an early draft. Also many thanks to my tutors at UEA, especially Andrew Cowan and Trezza Azzopardi.

I'm indebted to Writers' Centre Norwich for selecting me to receive an Escalator Award, and Midge Gillies for her mentoring help. Much support and encouragement also came from my fellow 2007 Escalator winners, particularly Liz Ferretti, Clare Jarrett and Guy Saville, who gave me feedback on various versions of the manuscript, and listened patiently to my whinges about writing.

I'd also like to acknowledge my agent, Jane Conway-Gordon, for her support and belief in *The Listeners*, as well as Anna Power, Rachel Calder and Sallyanne Sweeney, who provided valuable early feedback on the manuscript.

I'm extremely grateful to Lucy McCarraher and Rethink Press for choosing *The Listeners* as one of the winners of their New Novels Competition 2014; without Rethink *The Listeners* would, most probably, still be languishing on my computer. Credit is also due to my friend Clive Dunn for his wonderful cover photography.

Above all though, I'd like to thank my brother, Chris, for his encouragement and advice; Bailey for his constant companionship while writing the book; and Kirsty for her unstinting support. Finally, Flo, my late grandmother; childhood visits to her Norfolk home, with its neighbouring woods and meadows, have always stayed with me, and provided the inspiration for the novel's setting.

This book was written with the assistance of an Arts Council England grant.

ABOUT THE AUTHOR

Edward Parnell lives in Norfolk and has an MA in Creative Writing from the University of East Anglia. He is the recipient of an Escalator Award from Writers' Centre Norwich, and in 2009 received a Winston Churchill Travelling Fellowship to fund a seven-week book research expedition to the Australian Outback.

Edward has previously worked for BirdLife International and the Norfolk Wildlife Trust, and has written numerous natural history and conservation-related articles for magazines and newspapers; he has also worked extensively in television and media production. Currently, he is a freelance editor and copywriter.

The Listeners is his first novel.

Lightning Source UK Ltd.
Milton Keynes UK
UKOW02f2334010215

245460UK00003B/124/P